WITHDRAWN

D1024758

the spectacle
of the body

YOLO COUNTY LIBRARY
226 BUCKEYE STREET
WOODLAND, CA 95695-2600

noy holland

STORIES

the spectacle

of the body

SS.
HOLLAND

ALFRED A. KNOPF

NEW YORK

1994

HOLL COUNTY LIBRARY
324 BUCKEYE STREET
HOLLAND, CA 95355-4500

THIS IS A BORZOI BOOK
PUBLISHED BY ALFRED A. KNOPF, INC.

Copyright © 1994 by Noy Holland
All rights reserved under International and Pan-American Copyright
Conventions. Published in the United States by Alfred A. Knopf, Inc.,
New York, and simultaneously in Canada by Random House of Canada
Limited, Toronto. Distributed by Random House, Inc.,
New York.

"Absolution," "He Has Been to Macy's," "Delicious," "Boulevard,"
and "Amharic" have appeared in The Quarterly.

Grateful acknowledgment is made to Better Half Music and Edwin H.
Morris & Company for permission to reprint an excerpt from "Civilization
(Bongo, Bongo, Bongo)" by Bob Hilliard and Carl Sigman, copyright ©
1947 by Better Half Music and Edwin H. Morris & Company, copyright
renewed. All rights reserved. Used by permission of Better Half Music and
Edwin H. Morris & Company, a division of MPL Communications, Inc.

Library of Congress Cataloging-in-Publication Data
Holland, Noy.
The spectacle of the body : stories / Noy Holland.
p.   cm.
ISBN 0-679-40481-3
I. Title.
PS3558.03486S67   1994
813'.54—dc20   93-34640
CIP

Manufactured in the United States of America
First Edition

MOTHER

Greatest thanks to Gordon,

captain in all weather.

Thanks to Sam and Will and Tom,

to Lauren and Beth and the three Kates—

Schimel and Fincke and Walbert.

contents

absolution

Me and him, we're lovers. Sure, I know, he's a crazy motherfucker. And I'm the Banana Queen of Opelousas.

They say I'm the prettiest since Luana Lee. But you best clap your eyes on Jimmy—he is something, too. If you saw Jimmy down by the dirty river in his shiny turquoise truck, you'd say, *Jimmy Lucas, he's plumb got everything,* a dog in the back, banking turns, his Banana Queen right close. He'd lift a finger from the steering wheel, tip his head to mean something mean. It's the way my Jimmy is. I've seen it happen, I should know, I rode with him a lot.

Nights at the No Knees we ride to, Jimmy sets me up on the long bar. "Just look at you," he says to me, his eyes wild and proud. "You boys come on, take a look at her. She is the Queen of Bananas."

People know about me and Jimmy. Jimmy was the first, I swear it. When I try remembering, creosote comes back best—two coats tacky on the storehouse floor, black across my back and legs. Helps cure dry rot. Don't I know? I slapped it on myself.

Oh, I'd have been down there anyhow, watching the boys ice the trains. I tell you, it's too hot for work like that here in Opelousas. Those chunks were all of fifty pounds, nothing but hooks to hoist them with. Those boys, they were always bright with sweat.

I used to sit up in the big red oak, just sorting, my head lining up their half-bare bodies: Jimmy, Jasper, Isaac, Read. Jimmy, Isaac, Jasper, Read. Jimmy was the first, I swear it. "Hey, Jimmy," I sang out, real softlike, just enough for me and the birds. "Hey, Jimmy."

He was a sight to see, standing splay-legged on a silver car, sweat running rivers down his back. A round, ugly fellow would come dawdling along, sticking bananas for safety's sake. "Just don't seem quite right," he'd say, eyeing the mercury like somebody's momma. "Best load her up, she's hot."

After a spell, the peel he stuck went black inside as a bullet hole.

Oh, bananas.

Opelousas is the banana capital of the universe—

cars and cars, quick up from Mexico City. Good seasons, those boys worked all night, throwing ice down
the loud chute. Jasper always did the last of it. He
was the oldest and he'd been to prison. Mind you, I
hardly looked at Jasper. I wasn't bad as all that. I seen
his black arms bare, though, veins standing out like
hard-ons in church.

Momma like to drive me loopdy-looped as she is
about Jimmy. "My lover Jimmy," I say in front of
her. "My man Jimmy."

She don't stand for it. He's a no-count. He ain't
the hitching kind. He spits tobacco juice on her kitchen
floor, no two words about it. Oh, sweet Jesus, I know.
Jimmy's got a mean streak an acre wide that puts up
a fence around me, puts a little shiver in me like I just
better be ready, like expect the worst, because here
it's coming. But I like it.

I don't know.

I do.

When I started in on Jimmy, Momma like to pinch
my head off. I'd get my hair done up. "How could
you!" You could hear her across the county. "How
could you!"

Lord, my momma can carry on. Some nights she's
talking a blue streak upstairs, and I lie down, dying
for the train—all those explosions right in a row, and
the whistle like something to run from.

Maybe I'm a sinner to sleep naked like I do.

Some nights I dream of fire, running stark down Jefferson with the neighbors gawking. Some nights Momma comes in, pushes her hands around on me. "Child of my heart," she says to me. "Sweet sugar child, don't go."

Daddy left way back, took a liking to some Mississippi baby doll. Folks says it's Momma I favor. But Momma wasn't ever Banana Queen. She ain't the contestant type. She like to laid down and get run over when Daddy brought his hussy—that's what I call her, his hussy—home. I knew it already. One day, early from school, I spied them, out at the kitchen sink, her bent down like she was spitting up, red hair spilling every which way. Strike me dead if I lie. I saw him sticking himself in her. It's the gospel truth.

I never told Momma. But she knew, she knew. Daddy's hussy's got a swing any fool wants for his porch. Momma don't say nothing. She just smiles sweetlike, slow in the doorway waving. Just like the Banana Queen of Opelousas. Just like me.

Me, I aim to be remembered. That's why the Banana Queen. You can't believe how it's transporting. It hooked me Jimmy. I'd have set up in that red oak till *I* grew roots, hadn't been for this yellow crown. Luana Lee is milk soup. Did Jimmy Lucas bat an eye? But give me a crown on appointment night, and Jimmy climbs up, clamps his hands on my face. "Ain't you something," he says to me. "If you ain't a precious thing."

Momma says it'll teach me vanity, being a queen and all. She says it'll make me big for my britches. I say, "Momma? Tell me something I don't know already."

Momma's crazy, I can't help it.

Momma says when your life goes short, folks stop listening to you. "How many times do we get to do this?" she says.

She says, "Fetch me a glass of water."

I can't help it. I want to sleep in the woods in a queenly bed and lacquer my broken toenails. I want to dig through Jimmy Lucas. One day last summer, Jimmy set a stuffed doll astride a rail of fence. He took her to pieces, shot by shot, head first and feathers rising. I could see the inside of his mouth. The inside of Jimmy Lucas's mouth is a dark, vibrating place.

I know.

I don't look in Momma's mouth. She's got pretty lips, but she smells like dying. I bathe her in the mornings these days. I try to help her along. I set Momma down in her pink tub and she wraps her arms around my neck and whispers, "You should have killed me when you had a chance."

A couple years back, before I got to be queen, we were loading hay on the flatbed. This is what she means—that the Devil took hold, that I meant her to flip off the back of the truck, bales tumbling. Momma looks like that now, like she looked that day—shiny-eyed and barely breathing, a fuse fixing to blow.

Sometimes Momma wants my mouth on her breast, like when I was her child. I lay myself down beside her, inside the darkness underneath the spread. Sometimes I think it could do me in—our nakedness, that, in my mouth, I can feel her old heart pounding. I try to help her along.

Like to make Jimmy wild, hearing this. "Don't you touch that old whore," he says. "You got to have a life of your own."

It is all of it new to me. Everybody wants something I can't figure. Jimmy wants a baby and I say, Why? The sense of it quits me. We could get us a trailer on the outskirts of town, a place where a dog could run. I just say, "No, Jimmy, no, no, no. You know I can't, Jimmy, no."

He don't stand for it. He grabs me by my ankles and drags me around, my head swimming on the linoleum. "Fuck you, you bitch," he says to me. "Fuck you, you cunt."

He drags me around. When he comes down on me, I think I must look like Momma, all sprawled out, my head thrown back like I am coming on.

Jimmy ain't come around since Daddy come home, but he is all I can think of.

Daddy done run out of luck. We supposed he drowned in the dirty river when they found his old brown boots. But Daddy ain't been drowning, only getting fat.

"Where you been, Daddy?" I say through the screen.

He looks like some old boy I never knew in school.

"Oh, here and yonder. Best let me in."

But do you think I budge?

"What you been doing, Daddy?"

He gives a little shrug like *plenty*.

"Watching the grasshoppers spit," he says, and then just stands there, fatter than fat, sucking at the gaps in his teeth.

Momma sits bolt up in back of me, spewing linchpinned to the flagpole and fourteen million dollars. She is Queen of Nonsense now, and that gives her the right.

"She ain't saying nothing, Daddy. Don't mean a thing. What can I do for you?"

He says, "I just come to set for a bit."

I say, "Unh-uh, Daddy. Ain't no reason to live in hell and have to wind up there, too. Why don't you just get along?"

He is nothing but a shadow against the screen, and from where I stand, flies disappear in him. I say, "You had your chance, old man. Momma's got a thing with God now."

.   .   .

It is all I can do to keep my hands from myself. Jimmy come by, just shuffled up, kind of hanging his head, making a ghost on the screen. I've seen it happen, I knew it was come.

"Jimmy," I say, "how them bananas?"

He says, "I had me a dream. I was looking for you. I was down yonder on the blacktop ridge, hollering every way from Sunday. You wasn't hearing a thing. You was down in a long valley in a little old house with a white light. You was all prettied up and your lips were red and you was just setting, looking at me, not seeing a thing, not listening."

Ought to be something for a girl to say, but my mouth refuses me.

He says, "Come on, child. I can't dawdle around. I got me a life to live."

"Uh-huh," I say. "Tell me about it, lover boy."

"Tell me what it's like," Momma says to me. "Tell me what it feels like to feel like a queen."

"Momma," I say, "Kiwanis makes six hundred and twenty-eight pounds of banana pudding every year, and every year those boys come up from down the road a piece and go to pissing in the yellow vat. It feels a little like that, I guess—like everybody's happy to have you, but you got some secret stinking inside."

Anytime she finds sleep, Momma goes to smiling and kissing the air. I've got a notion she looks like me, practicing love in the glass. *Am I doing this right? Do I look okay?*

I been making ready since long back when, but—Momma, she can still turn me inside out. When she came up last night from that crazy spell, she took hold of my face like she ain't laid eyes maybe for years on me.

"Oh, my beloved child. I thought I was living forever in that green, tumbling place."

It was like I'd never seen her before, like she was the light of another world. "Here," she said. "Put your hand here."

I rested my hand on her belly—my hand pressed under Momma's hand. "I'm all of me gone from here. Feel?" she said. "Do you feel it?

"Listen," she said. "Don't matter nohow. It's God does the things that ever get done. God made them boys piss in the pudding, ain't nothing to do with you."

Father, forgive.

If I ever flew, it would feel like this, like the earth is just something long gone. I got a big heart and can hold my breath, and when I go deep in this dirty river, my whole body disappears. I can feel water wanting me. I know it's a sin, but I open my legs. I shout Jimmy's name so it turns to music by the time that it finds air.

Oh, ain't it a shame, my sweet, sweet Jimmy. I could have loved you good.

Father, forgive.

I lie in the woods in the heat for the train. The thing gets growing inside me, up in my gut, around and around my secret parts. It has a life of its own, and surely the hunger of a hundred horses. It is a thing of the flesh, child of the Devil, who split my momma's pretty lips and spilt himself in her. Surely now is the time for prayer.

Dear God, sweet God, pray God.

What's my momma ever done to you? You listen to me. Ain't no kind of life you're lending her.

I got the skirling sound of a train come smack between my ears. It goes, *Take me. Take me,* it goes. *Take me, take me, take me, take me.*

Do I have to do all your filthy work?

Have you spent up all your amazing grace?

You think I know better, but you got me wrong— I ain't afraid of you. You can have this no-count soul to keep. Suit yourself. Do what you will. Tickle me pink. I can't use it.

Glory be and to the Father, and to the Holy Son. I would let Momma sprawl on the shimmying track.

You got your doubts.

I'd say, *Go on, go on. Get on with it, Momma. Let's be done with this thing.*

he has been to macy's

So he went on down there.

He went there in his truck.

It rained.

Mrs. Finn was in the kitchen, kneading dough for her daily bread. Around her waist was a calico apron the mice had long since chewed through.

The last stretch, he walked, leaving his truck, with the rain coming in, at the edge of a vast cornfield. He had a sideways way of walking, the hind foot some way sluggish, likely to drag or skip. He was wearing a brown fedora, a linen jacket, a pair of just-shined shoes. He had shot two holes in the floor of his truck so the rain would run on through.

Flour bloomed from the top of the counter and clung to the skin of her arms. Hens laid eggs in the outhouse. It was a bad day for making bread.

He came through the tomato field, picking his way between the knocked-down stakes and the brown plants now bent over, a tangle where there were once neat rows.

Birds clung to the eaves of Mrs. Finn's house. The screen was missing from the big kitchen window. Onward he came, passing beneath the shelter of the big live oak, that great swooning creature of a tree whose limbs kissed the banks of the pond. Some Yankee, Mrs. Finn surmised.

The man knocked at the frame of the front screen door and received no answer. He had come too far for this. He would burn her out if need be. He knocked at the door again. Crocodiles fed on the banks of the pond. Something big swept down from the big live oak and beat the air above his head. Then came footsteps, such soft things, slippered feet on a bare wood floor.

But Mrs. Finn did not open the door. She watched the stranger through the fly-specked screen, her fingertips pressing against it. In this screen, there was a tear, torn by the wind that tore through here she could not remember how long ago. She cleared her throat before she spoke, leaned toward the man, pressing against the screen so hard that the skin of all ten of her fingertips bumped up through the grid.

"That's pneumonia weather," she said.

She pointed outside with her chin.

The man's tongue came out and, curling up, caught drops that fell from the fedora's brim. The tear in the screen tore toward both ends of Mrs. Finn's body.

"Leave them things on the porch now and come on in where it's dry."

The man's tongue was curled up into a ditch that the rain dropped into and ran down through. He stood there. He would catch her, too. He could see Mrs. Finn was going to dive through that screen, hands wide like that, leaning toward him, pointing her sharp chin.

Mrs. Finn cleared her throat again. She eased back, said nothing. Dustings of flour left on the screen showed where her fingers had been.

"Amend me," the man said. "I had thought your eyes blue."

He was sitting cross-legged on the bare wood floor, tapping his chin with his finger. Mrs. Finn's hands were in her lap. Her eyes were as bright as the eyes of a bird, but only the whites were blue— a pale blue, like the moon when it blues in a certain season.

"You are wondering why I have come," the man said. "What there is I can tell you."

There was a parrot on the screened-in porch, poking at the man's wet shoes. *Buenos dias,* it sang, *Howdy do.*

The man said, "I could tell it suchwise, missus— from Coney Island to my house."

He took a sip from the cup of tea Mrs. Finn had made for him. The parrot climbed into one shoe.

"It was dusk," the man said, "one wintry, one-color day. Where it was I had come back from, I can no longer recall. I had come in my usual way, expecting, as usual, no one. But there he sat on the steps of my home."

Palm fronds clashed past the missing screen of the big kitchen window. The smell of bread traveled the rooms.

"George had been out to Coney Island," the man said, "where Atlantia overtakes the land. There he swore the sky had swelled up above him. 'I lay on my back on the dirty sand and the sky came and laid down along me,' George swore, 'heavier than a woman and pleasanter, too, until I thought she would . . .'

"Ah," the man said. "You have your doubts. You have your doubts, I see that."

Mrs. Finn had pulled to the edge of her easy chair. She was fingering the hole in her apron.

"George assured me you would not, in the beginning, understand. Try to understand," the man said. "I present it to you as a single tale from Coney Island to my house. But George had been all over. He was a thoughtful man. George thought, Inside me is the Kingdom of Heaven.

"But even heaven scared George then. The bones of the roller coaster sang in the wind. Fish washed onto the dirty sand and rolled back into Atlantia again. Would heaven be like *this?* George feared. This rancid, tumorous gray? If this was how, after all, he looked inside, would this be his share of the Kingdom of Heaven?

"He said, 'Waves breaking easy on the dirty sand made a dim, high-slapping sound, like a great deck of cards being shuffled.'

"George palmed his chest, where the swelling was. 'How about,' he joked, 'a bit more color: cholera green, pneumonia blue, salmonella yellow?'"

Mrs. Finn crossed her legs at the ankles. From the fold of her apron in the space between her legs, both of her hands were lifted, pressed between the man's two hands like the pages of a book he might read. The man knelt up. How pale his face was. Mrs. Finn felt herself being prayed to, though it made no sense to her why. The man kissed the tips of her fingers.

"Listen, little bird. A small sleep," he said, "a small slumber, and the memory of him is me."

The man's hands slipped so softly from hers that Mrs. Finn's hands were left praying.

The rain let up; the house grew quiet. A crocodile slid into the pond.

The man sat back on his haunches and, hearing

the hard weight of him against the bare wood floor, Mrs. Finn brought her knees together, and she stood, and sure that she was not watching him, instead the man listened, such soft things, those footsteps, going away and gone now and coming back again.

When Mrs. Finn came back into the room, the man was in George's easy chair, the one chair in the one room the wind had not walked through, picking and choosing from among their things. Mrs. Finn sat down on the floor on the cushion she had brought for the man to sit on. The man poured the last of the tea, though it had gotten cold by then, into a cup, which Mrs. Finn drank from.

"Suppose this," he began again. "Reckon that when the Beginning began, Our Father exploded. Our Father art tiny trillions of pieces riding above the world.

"His was a strange pilgrimage," the man said, "your George's was. He caught the next train to Manhattan. George thought, If I believe in one God, and that God exploded, does it not stand to reason, then, that in the Beginning there was one man—one set of eyes and arms and legs, one heart, one head—and that he, too, exploded?

"Suppose that the world is a single body where each man's pain is every man's sorrow, where each man, created in a shattered God's image, jettisoned into the stratosphere by the force of a huge explosion, came falling upon the earth.

"That makes so many ways of fitting together, and only so many pieces."

The man leaned toward Mrs. Finn, bending away from the back of the chair, the joints of his hips creaking.

"See my hands," he said. "Look here."

Mrs. Finn held his hands in both of her hands. She turned and turned them over. "And these, too," the man said, leaning ever more, his eyes so close to Mrs. Finn's eyes that their eyelashes were almost touching.

"These are your husband's eyes," he whispered. "I know all about you, duckie. I have been all over."

Mrs. Finn lighted a candle between them. The last of the sun had gone from the sky and left not the crimson of frequent evenings, but a fat, dank, catholic gray, noticed not by Mrs. Finn nor by Mrs. Finn's stranger, talking on as he did in small ways a stranger now to outside things, talking against the silence that pressed against their lives.

The stranger lowered himself from the easy chair and sat bent-kneed beside Mrs. Finn on the bare wood floor.

At the edge of the pond, in a halm of reeds, a cat stalked dragonflies, beetles.

Again the man spoke, and again, though he himself seemed not aware of it, a change usurped his voice.

"I have been where George has been, only not so

far, not quite so far as George is now, but elsewhere, yes, all over. I have been to Macy's," said the stranger, rocking now so fast on his haunches that Mrs. Finn placed her hand on his arm, desperate to calm him.

"I know all that George knows, more and less," he said. "How things cost you an arm and a leg, catch your eye, spin your head. I know about fathers who say to you, 'Son, I couldn't do without you; you know you're my right-arm man.'

"But, duckie? When George's father died out, George himself kept walking."

The man lowered his mouth to Mrs. Finn's hand, still calm against his arm. With his teeth, he tugged at her wedding ring. With his tongue, he parted her fingers.

"There is a man near Macy's," he said, "who sells plastic birds for a dollar. His one sleeve hangs empty. 'Hey, mister! When you fill 'em with water, they sing!'

"This got George thinking. His head swam with thoughts. If you lost an arm, was George's way of thinking, if you had to do without, then was there not some way, if you one day decided you could not keep on doing without, to go ahead and find your man and get your arm right back again? Was your arm, after all, not a body walking, stopping at storefronts, selling things on the corners of streets? Or if not, was it maybe a body still falling, a body you would find in the Kingdom of Heaven, in a place where, finally sorted through, everybody looked like you?

"When your own body betrays you, parts of you keep living with living people's bodies. For the people who are whole, there are parts of you left. There is a web of the parts of you left that the people you love will know about.

"Do you see now why I have come?"

The stranger carried the bird into the kitchen and filled it with water at the kitchen sink. Hens were coming out of the outhouse, white beyond the palm fronds, beyond the missing window screen, just shapes as far as the man could see, not seeing the twist and tilt of their heads as they heard him, him blowing through that bird a cock's crow; Mrs. Finn heard the man crow, too, her head, too, tipped over, perched again in George's easy chair, and then the *coo* that was like the coo of a dove that the parrot on the porch failed to parrot, giving off something more of a *caw* and, Mercy, Mrs. Finn thought, this with what was now so mercilessly the crunkling of a crane in the kitchen, the parrot failing at this as well, calling out *coo* instead, the parrot calling *coo coo ricoo*.

The cat trod circles on the screened-in porch.

The man squatted, set the bird beside Mrs. Finn on the arm of her easy chair. The weight of his heart he gave her, and also of his head, his forehead resting against her knees. She had her sister's knees, he knew. His breath passed between them.

" 'My heart,' he said, 'has gone out of it. My heart, I can tell you, is my Martha running through a door of glass. You must understand why I've come,' George said. George took off his hat and his linen jacket and he set aside his shoes."

The man slipped off Mrs. Finn's slippers. He rolled down Mrs. Finn's knee-high stockings and pulled them past her feet.

" 'Please,' he said. 'Give Martha my love.'

"He loved you very much, you know. He sent me with his love," the man said.

The bird let out a broken scream, its plastic tail caught between Mrs. Finn's lips; her legs, like two wings, parted.

The man nuzzled her cheek, her tiny mouth. She bit him.

"Are ye livin' in the shadder of the cross?" she whispered.

She could smell George's smell on his clothes.

"Shadder of the cross," the man whispered.

"Shadder of the cross," he said.

orbit

At night, we kept watch for turtles. We made our beds one bed to lie across together, our pillows pushed up in the window we had popped the screen from. There was a broken place in our yard, and in our yard, our garden. We could lean up onto our pillows at night and watch out over the garden.

This was in the yellow house; it was swallowed up by trees. Vines grew into the kitchen.

This was the summer our father left. Our mother lay at the back of the house.

There were trains at night, and whippoorwills, and

the sounds our mother made at night went out across our yard. We moved Mother's bed to the window— so she could see the sun and moon, so she could see the garden.

We let the animals harvest the garden—the mule deer and the whistle pigs, the rabbits nosed through our broken place—the things you have to kill to catch. It was easy, catching turtles. We leaned into the light from our window. My brother whistled a marching call to tease the turtles two-by-two: Sugar and Vernon, Oscar and Doll. That was what Orbit had named them. Every turtle we caught, we caught again. We carved their names with a crooked nail in the soft shells of their bellies. Our own names, we carved in the trees.

We named our bird dog Bingo then. Our father had named her Jane. We let her come sleep in our room with us, in our beds, underneath our bedsheets, her head on Orbit's pillow. We kept Bingo's tail in our pockets. Our turtles, we kept in a wooden box, or we let them loose in our mother's room before we carried them back out into our woods so we could catch them over again. We kept their box beneath our beds so we could hear them if they moved at night.

We heard Mother sing at night—Mother Goose and birdcalls. Whenever she was singing, when we could not help but hear her singing, Orbit flung the bedsheet back and went out through the window. I went to Mother with saltines, Popsicles, to feed her. She pulled the bedsheet up across her mouth, held it below her eyes, and danced, veiled—her arm dipping above the sheet, her hand fluttering out at the end of it. I heard her hips twist.

I heard the field mice, shredding her clothes, in the dresser.

When Orbit came back with his bike from the lake, I sneaked to our bed and pretended to sleep—so he could wake me, so we could hunt for turtles. Some nights he did not wake me. He curled under his sheet at the foot of his bed, and I would feel our beds rock; I would hear the box springs start to shudder and creak and our bird dog—curled up at the edge of the bed—moaning, her head underneath Orbit's pillow. I pulled the sheet over my head to listen—to his hand pumping his tiny prick, to him breathing.

Orbit brought jars of tadpoles from the lake, scooped from the weedy shallows, and frogs, gigged and bleeding, he tried in the coming days to heal. He sewed up the frogs with needle and thread, patched their lesser wounds with gauze, practiced amputations.

Without Mother, we broke rules.

We ate with our fingers, if we ate at all. We said, *Fingers were made before forks.*

We put tadpoles underneath our beds with the World Books, the box of turtles.

We popped the screen from our window—so we could lean out over our windowsill so we could watch for turtles. When our wonder beans swung, there were turtles. Orbit was feet-first, shouting *Geronimo!*, dropping past the windowsill before his bedsheets settled. He kicked away from the side of the house, lunging backward, gaining yard to the garden.

This is what was; this is what can have been.

We were Queen Mother and Orbit, we said, the summer she lay at the back of the house, the autumn, the spring. Our father was other places. Our father had sat with his hat at his feet, useless in the kitchen. When he stood up, he stood up walking, moving to the door.

We did not try to stop him.

We do not try to stop him.

We are Queen Mother and Orbit of the night birds and the terrapin, of the tubers and of the leaving trees.

We are a ruckus of arms in the head-high weeds, bent-kneed, dropping to stalk on our fingertips between the rows of corn. In the squash, we drop to our hands and knees and then to our bellies—elbowing, dragging our legs, too loud in our own moving sounds to hear past ourselves for prey. We watch down the rows for the beans to swing; we keep an eye on Bingo, who is standing on the windowsill, watching over us from our room. We have her broken-off tail in our pockets, and rabbit's foot in our pockets, and the crooked nail we name them with—our Sugar, our Vernon, our Doll. Oh, we are so lucky! So grown, how blessed, such seers!

We stop in the dirt to listen.

We know Mother watches for us. We are sure she is listening for us. There are strays, after all, wilding fields, and fire—and we have seen houses splintered by wind lift like leaves from their yards.

We listen for the closing up, the hinged, hydraulic sound of the keeping shells of the turtles. Orbit howls and I, Mother and I, watch him—cat-backed, my brother, a boneless pounce of boy into a sprawling thicket. He thrashes through the vines and leaves; we see a flash of scrawny arm, a ratty patch of hair. A sorrowful moan leaves Bingo, her havocked, swallowed trill. We see my brother's legs jerk straight, Mother and Bingo and I—then nothing; then he lies with his feet poked out of the beans as though he has been grown over.

"It's Sugar," he explains to me, and hands off the turtle.

A green moon is the best moon, Orbit claims, for turtles.

Our mother claims in a green moon, as rare by far as a blue moon, our father comes home and carries her out and, hand over hand, runs her up the flagpole in our yard.

We hear her pleading with the Pope at night, blind-gigging geese at night.

We have our Gander in our yard, our trough for frogs and tadpoles.

Sugar we have—and Oscar, soon to knock at our legs in our pockets.

Orbit claims that if they would let you, held open against your ear, you could hear the sea in Sugar, in Oscar, and so on—in turtles we have not yet caught to let us listen to them there. Sugar is cool underneath, where the shell smooths and smells to me of potatoes. Our potatoes, left to freeze, will grow hard as bone in winter, food for vole and shrew. Turnips we grow for their smooth skins swelling in the press of earth; beets for their rough, knuckly peel we peel back in bed with our kitchen knife in our room I was first to be born in, our yellow house stooped and winded as far from town as from the sea.

Pitchfork,
Moon Pie,
tarpaulin,
Lipton's,
hangers to mend the fence,
morphine—

Not the sea I hear in Sugar, but my brother saying *penknife,* Orbit saying *saltines* to put on the list for supper. But town is a long and, even in the cool, blistering walk through the hollow. We keep near her, Mother on a good day taking toast and tea, a day when the sound she makes at night is not Mother Goose but Mother, the words we know of her, her calling over the windowsill my brother and me by name.

Night to night, day to dark, very night of very night,
Orbit recites to the undershells as white as the buffed
soles of our feet come bootless to the turtles. We learn
in the dark with our fingers what, with a crooked nail
and a kitchen knife, by candlelight we have named
them.

We take our time to name them. We lie with our
chins hanging past the edge of our twin beds. Turtles
are shy when they open, the swung-down half of a
moon of shell a ramp the kept inside of them might
lift up and walk out over. In me, also, is a flap of shell,
hinged, according to Orbit, open when I squat to pee
and, when I am finished peeing, drawn shut accord-
ingly ahead of the hooked and wrinkled neck the size
of Orbit's thumb, and mine; the skin of a turtle's neck,
as the skin of our mother's neck, is fit to be shed at
the side of a road, our mother not a mother to sing
before this jack-in-a-box of cheeks rouged with the
skin of beets we peel to pop out when we want her.
And we want so much of Mother.

In bed, the dark between our sheets keeps the smell
of lumped dirt, of crops we have left, of Mother—if
we touch her before we leave, or when we come back
to her from the garden. We smell ourselves of the
garden. We smell of Bingo—who smells of her kill
she has left in the woods and who sleeps her dog's
sleep with her head underneath Orbit's pillow.

Orbit's pillow, since our father left, has become
our dog's pillow; Bingo's name we changed from the
name we never liked all along. The nights since then,

since Father left, the nights our mother is singing, Orbit curls at the foot of his bed, thinking I am sleeping. But I am not sleeping. His boy's breath I am of him and of the fallen dark with him. I am the keeping sheath of him, slipping on his penis.

I see him reach his hand out. I see him turn his hand to let our Bingo lick it clean.

We try to lure the turtles out with shiny slugs and straight-pinned flies, with the luck of rabbit's foot saved frozen from the garden.

We are lucky when they open.

They are so shy.

We try to pry them out with kitchen knives and pliers, to burn them out with candles, mute things, toothless. Do they know it when we sleep? Do they rise up in their old homes and walk out in our room at night?

But we are not sleeping.

Maybe they dream.

Might it be not the sea we hear but of some lurching, yellow dream we wake to keep from dreaming?

I am no weak sister gone kneeling through the house at night to harvest lint from carpets, to polish and to clean. I am not afraid to sit darkly among our things and in the room where Mother sleeps, or is not sleeping, to sing, or am not singing.

But I do not sleep with Mother, shall not when she lifts the sheets and pats our father's place to lie against her in their bed.

Our beds are one bed, my brother's bed and my

bed. We lie across together. But I would go, should Mother call—between this room and that, between sister and daughter. Or if she does not call, I will go to sit and watch her dreaming.

You will know the place, should you ever come, as soon as you have seen it. You will see it from the dirt road—the house leaning, and leaning, slumped, from the narrowing wind from the hollow.

Should the stone in the road you are walking past lift up on its legs and move, pick it up. It may be Vernon.

The spotted dog is Bingo, her paws webbed for swimming.

The goosenecked goose is Gander, hitched with a rope to the trailer hitch.

And the swaybacked mare—what of her? She lay in the grass behind the barn that stands beyond the slumping house and squeezed out her dead filly.

And of the mother?

And of the father—what shall we say of him?

It will be done as soon as the father comes or not—until he comes. The father will come by train or truck as fathers betimes are wont to come. Or by some flight of fancy.

Or he will not come.

Or he did not go, and shall not go, but stayed in Tuscaloosa.

Tuscaloosa is a good town. There are fathers in Tuscaloosa. There are no cars in Tuscaloosa, no guns, no books, no telephones, no telephone books to finger through waiting for dark to come. Or do you not wait for it? Or do you live in Little Crab? Mightn't you live in Oneida? Might you not wait for a father to come, driving himself in a vented rig with a feather alight on the bill of his cap in the dash-light light of the cab of his truck, driving chickens by night to Oneida?

I was born in Ohio.

My mother was someone, chances are, I never might have known.

Do you know Oneida? Would you take my word for what I would tell you about Oneida?

Ask anyone.

Ask my mother.

Is it pretty somewhere near Oneida?

Is there a boy you know named Orbit living on the outskirts there?

Ask yourself any old thing you might think of to want to ask yourself, or not to want to ask yourself. Will it be done, for instance, when it is done? In a whimper, will it? In a heartbeat?

Old Mother Hubbard lived in a cupboard covered with pudding and pie. *Who saw her die? Who saw her die?*

It was I, said the fly, *with my little teensy eye.*
Who caught her blood? Who caught her blood?
It was I, said the fish, *it was I, in my pretty silver dish.*

❧

When Daddy comes, Orbit claims, I will show him.

I will show how in the tree, turning above the dogs, we keep the filly safely there to show him when he comes. The lean-to, I will show him. I will show him the broken place where the animals come into the yard.

Do you know where Turkey is?

How does a turnstile work?

Turtles have been toothless for one-five-zero, zero-zero-zero years.

This one is Oscar. Oscar, meet Doll. Daddy and Doll, meet Oscar. After a single mating, Doll can lay fertile eggs for years. Will they all at a time break open?

She will not show them. Our Doll will not show to me even her belly still. And if she is not with them? If our Doll is old and gray and nodding by the road one night, who will there be to show them? And which way goes to the paved road and on to the yonder sea?

I have not seen it. I have not seen the sea.

I see crows.

I know there are buzzards banking turns up there.

I keep the flies from Momma. It is my job to keep them from her. The sky is yellow. The fields and the fields and the fields are green. The lean-to is blue. My name is Orbit.

"Oh, you're that little Gibson boy with buckeyes in his britches."

"Momma," I say, "it's Orbit."

But who am I to tell her? Who am I to Momma? What am I to say?

For luck, I shook a buckeye down to clatter from our buckeye tree. She put it in her mouth.

Our dog is Bingo. We gave Bingo Bingo. Bingo is a dog's name. We took Jane away.

So is it Jane's or Bingo's tail we worry in our pockets?—broken, ropy, gyplet tail Daddy cut away. So maybe it is Daddy's. But it is in our pockets. Our goosenecked goose is Gander. If Gander is our Christmas goose, will we take his name away? And will it still be Christmas? Will Daddy come to carve the goose when she is dead who took his name and with it died away?

Sometimes I cannot hold my breath for Momma's long not-breathing. I keep her sheet snugged under her. *One Mississippi,* I count. *Two, three Mississippi. Four.*

Outside is the garden.

My bike is in the garden.

I hold my breath between our breaths so she will not stop breathing. But sometimes I breathe. I cannot keep from breathing. There is the lean-to. There are birds to clean. There is the light to think of. Already the day is so long past the coins sun-dropped through the leaves of the trees of the locusts calling *Phaaaraoh,* past jarflies and dragonflies that stitch the air above our lake, our house shadow flung as far and wide as both our yard and garden.

Still there is no sign of my sister.

But surely she will come.

Cissie will want to be the one when Momma wakes up screaming, and Momma wakes up screaming— *What time is it? Oh, let me up! I have got to get into that kitchen!*

But there is only sun-time here, and the fickle moon in the trees at night, and the months that pass from the things that bloom and that are rotten in the garden.

There are wonder beans now; there are turtles.

Upon a time the times we did not sleep, Daddy shunt the hall at night to lock us in our room at night when we were not sleeping. There is no lock to lock now. Now is the door and the hall and the door any boy can follow. You can see our house at night. We leave the porch light on at night. You can see it burning. Once Daddy came to our room at night when I was afraid of the dark at night, of the night sounds and the dogs at night and in the woods the cows at night, though days I saw them feeding. Then I did not sleep with Oscar then; then Cissie's bed was one bed and my bed another. I did not sleep with Bingo. Then Bingo slept on the floor of our room, before she slept at the head of my bed, before the two-dollar truck would run, before she got my pillow. Now it is Bingo's pillow. Now it is Bingo's tail for me to finger in my pocket.

I am not a scaredy. Only but to shoo the flies a boy would need to look at her. I am small to bathe at her or to try to keep her eating. But I am not a scaredy. I am like my daddy. My bike is in the garden. My lamp is in the bread box. My straw, my shreddy shoes.

And I am in the garden. My bike is in the porch light lying in the garden. My feet are in my shoes. Whooey.

Cornstalks left and splinted peas, the scrabbly path that splits our yard, oh fast, our moon, the window left, our porch light left on burning late for Daddy not to come, or to come when I am hiding, sly as sly Geronimo, snakely in the tree limbs hung with copperheads and squatting cranes that ghost across our lake at night.

Nights!

Oh, the tree frogs!

What boy was I to be afraid ever of the tree frogs? Ever of the blat and twang, the rasp and scraw and cruck of things—the warbling, the mournful, the trees, the leaves fallen all hushened to a churchly calm to keep me up with Daddy? I kept up with Daddy. Daddy creaked like trees. Daddy smelled like creosote slathered on the wooden shed, the leaning fence, the barn my bike thrums and rattles past—a swift bank, a cock-kneed swoop he showed me—house and barn and creekbed gone, turtles gone, a moon, a stunt to make my momma gasp to get down to Daddy, to hold her breath for Daddy—no hangdog on the fence we built to fence the bending hill we built the barn to squat on, no spotty clerk, my daddy, not a man to cobble shoes. Did he not know the names of things to call the nightly sounds by? By Cricket, by Screech Owl, by Croaker?

My way is quick: the barn, the slough, the hidden field. My way loops through the hidden field, between the vaulting stalks of weeds so near you have to hold my breath to hold my bike to ride by—to stoop, unmooned, no smoothened pass, but the sting and smeary green of greening knees to steer by.

My name is Orbit.

Joe Pye, Milkweed, Mullen.

The lake is low. My bike is old. You can hear it coming. In the leaves are cans to kick where I have tipped my bike down.

My lamplight is on. My Dixie straw, my gigging prong, my knack I have among the trees for soggy calculation, my skinny pole, my skiff I have to stand up in to skinny by the trees by night by night-blind navigation.

I hear such frogs.

They fall to feeding when I pass them. But I do not pole past them. I shine my light across them—long of toe and yellow-eyed and wide mouths to pry open. Slow now, and soft to go. You have to go so soft as me to catch them in the laps of trees, gawky in your narrow boat in the lapping shallows. The weak place is the white place that bloats out when they call. They flap and bleed when you gig them.

I let Bingo taste them. I let Bingo lick my hands when I have slicked my hands at night. But I do not croon. I do not pitch and moan to see our Cissie curl her toes underneath our sheets at night when Momma is still singing, and Momma is still singing. Momma is always singing.

I pry their mouths open.

I scrape my straw down into them—and breathe.

The green-headed and the long-legged and the blackflies hatched in the spit-gobbed trees tick by day at our windows. Inside the flies are flies inside and in the frogs flies inside and in our house also and also in Bingo worms inside—hook and whip and ringworm worms and worms left to feed in Bingo's heart—pale, mute, sluggish, plumping in the bloody rush in the blinding heart dividing.

We have lakes to swim. We have trees.

The heart, like an egg, a heart, has been known, her heart, like an egg, to break open.

Surely it will not break open.

Momma will not break open. The filly did not break open.

I cut the filly with a carving knife to turn above the dogs at night safe from the limb of our tree—and when Daddy comes home, I will show him. I will show him the broken place where the animals come into the yard.

Bingo comes into the garden. Bingo is Bingo. But when Daddy comes, Bingo is Jane. But tonight is tonight. Tonight is the light of a greening moon a boy can see to ride by, and else to ride to sea by. Daddy will not come tonight—when Momma is still singing, when Bingo is not Jane.

My sister's name is Cissie. Our momma's name is Cissie.

You can hear us calling. You can see our house at night. We leave the porch light on at night.

You can see us calling.

There is the dirt road, the paved road, the airport. Should we walk to the dirt road, we could not hear her screaming. Should we walk to the paved road, we could not see the porch light. But should we walk to the airport?

If we cannot hear her screaming, if we cannot see the porch light, no porch, we can see no house at night, no dogs to see who run their dreams beside our father's bed at night now that we are leaving, and we are leaving. The dirt road that starts at the graveyard, or ends, if you wish, at the graveyard, and begins, if you wish, at the paved road, to take us to Oneida, to take us to Tuscaloosa, takes us out in the snow some night to walk the rising tide some night until our hats start floating.

But that is not our want, we claim. After all that we have claimed of it, this seems not the road at all.

Oh, but I dissemble.

There is a yellow house I know set back from a road I know. There is a well there. From the well comes the sweetest water.

We have no bucket. Shall we assume, then, the well is dry? Shall we say there is no well at all, no yellow house, no mother? And if a mother, what shall we say of her—that she is pretty? That she is quick to dance a Charleston in her rhinestone shoes? Very well, then. She was pretty. She was quick to dance a Charleston in her rhinestone shoes.

Shall we make a claim from up on airship high how the road comes to look not a road at all but a rope to knot a loop into to kick a chair out under from, or from yellow porch to pin oak tree to pin a mother's trappings from?—her gold lamé, her taffeta, her brocades flown across the sea or boated in a ribboned box

from some shop we have not thought to think of yet
in Hong Kong—her girdles, Mother's hard brassieres,
her gowns back-slit with a kitchen knife we hand over
hand to fly by night—greenish, blooded, nylon—
usurers, children, thieves—her nylons to pull past our
chins at night to steal from our mother's room at night
that we might well be on our way, well down the road
I would not claim as clothesline or hangman's noose,
no ribbon to bewitch in a young girl's hair to flurry
by chance in your slowing rush on the old road, or the
new road, the dirt road, the paved road, headlong to
get to Ohio.

It would please me to think you might think of
me as a girl you picked up driving once, or thought
to pick up driving once, who says, as we ride, nearly
nothing. That we have met perhaps in a dream you
might think. That we have eaten pork chops—this
would please me. That we have left the last bright
diamond field, the shrinking glare of hamburger joints,
of car lots and Circle K's, dog tracks and Sears.

You are so pretty.
Is there nothing I can say to you?
Is there not a vein you love lashed beneath your
mother's skin she lets you fiddle with your fingers?
Must you follow with your fingers the broken and
the boldened roads, the turnpikes, the highways, the

lists made of names of towns to go to sitting beside your mother's bed for the last breath breathed out at the back of the house?

You may go now.

But will you come back?

Will you not come to hear her calling you late from the wide field, from your hay forts and your strewn caves—the thin rain, the cities?

The cities flee from my windows.

I do not rest much. A run of music, a plain door, in the hard streets the sound of horses sends me on.

I push on.

Sometimes a door opens.

Sometimes with some man spent in me, Mother comes to me tugging her catheter, the limp, blooded tip of it, out from where I have forced the tube into Mother's—I want to say—womb.

Is it possible to be gentle?

Her skin is a yellow bruise.

Mother dents where you touch her.

I am like her. Each day I am more like her. I have her hands, my mother's mouth, her long, straight body.

Go fuck yourself, Ohio.

We tied our mother by our wrists with scarves and to the bedstalks by our ankles. We had a great stash of morphine, a run of hot nights of a sweetened cast that clotted in our throats. We had gizzards. We grew scales. We had feet. We were bottom-feeders.

We were flat out over our lake by night with each a stone to ride by. Our stones grew smooth. They sunned all day. We found it warm to hold them. We eased the stones over the rim of our skiff and the water rose on the flank of our skiff and rose again for my brother. Our skiff nosed up and flattened. Our skiff nosed down and flattened. We had chosen each one stone. We held them. It was all we could do to hold them. We tipped, tucked over, dropped ourselves into the water.

All the moon long, we fell. The stones rode against our bodies. Past breathing, unshapened things we fell past. It was pleasing. Our lives grew strangely pleasing. We were told the lake had no bottom. It was said the lake had no bottom. Our lives grew strangely pleasing. Such creatures—whiskered, feeding things, shelled things—we bumped past. We came upon the lake's dark bottom.

Did you think we would die of it, Mother?

Everywhere was a bruise on her, and the flecked wounds of our needles. Her bones scraped under her skin—we could hear them, when she moved at all, when we helped her turn in bed. We turned her to salve the widening sores that mouthed out from the weight of her bones, from the weeks, the months she lay there.

We brought pretties. We brought her things to smell. We brought our mother bits of things she used to think to speak of. There were smoothed things—leviathan, terrapin, Pawnee. We moved along the silted bottom. Our hearts thrilled in our ears.

She waked up screaming.

Orbit waked up screaming.

The sky stayed the same pale haze.

Her cookware and cameos, a deck of cards, her cigarette box, needles, nylons we buried out in the garden. We dragged our beds to the garden. Sometimes we sang.

We brought slingshots. We had Bingo and kitchen knives, a certain native know-how. The days grew dusty. The fields were tipped with ocher. We bound our mother with her bright scarves by her wrists to her bed, by her ankles. Our beds we dragged to the garden. Our turtles scuffed in the garden. We had shards of pot and bone, rabbit and whistle pig; dogs dug under our broken fence to nose over us in our garden. Mother called out. Bingo chewed up her slippers. Bingo chewed up a rhinestone shoe Mother used to dance the Charleston in—years back, or days back, should you ask her. Ask her would she show us, and Mother would be our scissor knees, our wild arms on the screen porch, a thumbnail, some harvest, any old green or fish-belly moon it would be our want to ask her.

We planted the rhinestones two by two with a foot between in the garden. We grew. We were still growing. We carved our names in our arms. No rain came, no father. Orbit stayed out in the garden. I would leave Orbit out in the garden. A house is so dark inside when you have been out in the garden. I wore bracelets of leaves. Her gold lamé, I wore it.

"Mother," I said, "it's me."

"If you say so," she said.

I said, "We were out in the garden."

"I see. And what did you sow?" she said. "I've seen no moon to plant by."

"No moon, Mother. No motherlight. By twos we planted bright stones to lead us out from the garden."

"Stones, child?"

"Stones, Mother."

"And what of your mother, child?"

"We will dig her a hole in the garden."

"And how will you face her, child?"

"As I do, Mother. With a difference."

"Then face her south, then. But will you bind her?"

"No, Mother."

"But you will face her? Will you build for her a simple box that the dirt not burst her eyes?"

"If you wish, Mother."

"Are you certain, child? What wonders the dead accomplish. But the living? Oh, uncalmable, a palsied, mewling sack. To breathe, I am cinched and watered. This is a child's love, child? Child, you call this love, child? Love?"

. . .

We could see her from the garden. We tied rabbits by loops of string to cornstalks in the garden. We kept Gander. We filled a trough for frogs.

I held her. It was all I could do to hold her. "You are trying to kill your mother," she said. "Are you trying to kill your mother?"

Underfoot is a millet of bone. The road opens out in a graveyard. Will you drive on? Have you not seen me? Do you see that they cut us bone to bone to sort through what might grow in her as we had grown in Mother? The wound gapes, leaks bile. Mother cannot swallow. Mother's veins collapse. For months the doctors come and go back out into Tuscaloosa. For months I will not lie with her and then one day I lay with her and in the nights thereafter and after a time to lie there, curved into the wound in her, I think to grow in under her, bone by bone, my toothy spine her long wound's tongue and groove to seal her. I think, if ever he comes to her, my father will come to feel me there if ever my father should touch her, and to feel me I think would please my father as I pleased my father once, my chipped spine my mother's skin will come to overgrow in her.

I can make her please him.

I rouge her cheeks, tease her hair, her slack sex sponge clean.

He will feel me. Our father cannot but feel me—

a bone-hard nub of bone in the soft, in the bowly hot suck and leech and long swim of Mother.

Get me out of here. Unmother me.

Oh, the airports of Ohio. There are salt bluffs in Ohio, roads to take run slick by rain to drive into my Ohio—these wasted acres walked off, strewn caves, my caverns scraped, stripped mines, ravines.

I cannot get free of her. She is tongued, gashed, towered. A door will open. She finds me eating. She finds me lacking. I am in some mall or lobby, some truck stop or Sears, six-stone set in some riverbed, she finds me. She finds me on the road some night as like as not in your rig some night where we have maybe swung wide in the gone seas of Ohio.

Listen, you. You, Einstein. Hum up, boy.

But there is more. There is always more. There is yet light enough, and always some motel out here with walls as thin as ice, enough breath: night: talk enough to kick a stone to town.

Let the sun so top the trees, it sits on a boy's head like a cap he has long since lost the thought of, thinking, *Pitchfork, Moon Pie, tarpaulin, Lipton's*—a boy to count and count again the worn heads of the silver coins singing in his pockets.

It may be that you know him, knowing enough at all events to conjure a name to call him by when the road from out of the hollow climbs to widen in the shut-down, dead heart of Oneida. Or maybe it is not Oneida. Maybe you know some farther town his daddy drove through in a two-dollar truck to find what who could guess at, what would only ever anyway be but a name Orbit guessed at, spelled out, this boy— the names with his momma's knitting needle scrawled across his sister's skin they could get the clothes pushed off of, Cissie's back bared and arms, her legs, her girl's skin given to rash and welt—so that riding back in the back of the truck with their momma's hair pulled back to them, a boy could dig down far enough for the names of the towns to welt enough for a careful tongue—for this boy's tongue—to follow.

It takes so little to please me.

I think of Orbit in the back of the truck thinking, *Slow,* I think to his daddy, but saying only to his sister, *Cissie, faster,* saying, *Make it go faster*—as though she, as though a person might so surely will the body as to will the letters of the towns gone through to sink from the unsunned white of her skin too long to Orbit's mind lasting—with the towns coming on, and dusk coming on, and with the saltiness of his sister's skin, the first faint taste of blood.

I think of them in the bed of the truck with the spare wheels and the empty cans, the crap their daddy took with him that leaves a left boy thinking—leaves

Orbit, thinking on the stone-kicked road that splits the long hollow how small, how truly stowable, a boy like him might prove to be to be among the what all a man with an eye to head for town might have picked and taken.

In time, his daddy will come. They will mend in time the broken place by now so long by lost dogs, mule deer, and so on, so long by now worked through that the greased hairs even of the whistle pigs fly from the fence curled back to a wire-toothed snarl.

All day, the porch light burns, all night, and of late by now, room by room, in the windowed rooms the lights of the house come up also, so there is light throughout also—a tall house, storied—light enough that, driving by, you are apt to let your window down to listen out for dancing, a glimmer of voices, some bit coming across the field of some familiar song.

But, quick now. Drive on. They have already seen you passing.

❧

As soon as Momma goes to sleep, I go back to Momma's room to light the light back burning. Momma dreams. The wind creaks the pin oak tree grown up in our yard at night and you can hear the dogs at night and sometimes someone's car goes by unlighted, with its engine off if I am in the garden.

My bike is in the garden. Nights when the wind and the moon come up, its spoked wheels turn.

I am growing tadpoles.

There are three-hundred and sixty-five different kinds of tadpoles. I keep a trough filled up for them to grow up in in the garden.

Cissie sits out in the garden. Soup pots, she sits with, and wooden spoons, lipsticks, purses, the lipped ends of cigarettes snubbed out in the corner drawer, the drawer—she takes even it to the garden, the scarves in it and soft-skinned gloves that, by and by, Bingo will find and bury again in the garden. Cissie drags our beds to the garden, her bed and my bed, so at night I sleep under Momma's bed and sit by day at the foot of her bed to see myself what the day will bring for Cissie to take to the garden.

She wears one hat one day and leaves it out the next day to come inside for another.

Some are feathered.

On some of them, the brims are wide the wind bends up.

The snubbed ends of the cigarettes Momma keeps in her corner drawer, Cissie takes in her corner drawer to smoke on in our garden. But they are still our momma's. I say to Momma, "Nome."

I know Momma sees out. But I say, "Nome."

I say it is not the pearly crown our momma bought to marry in when Cissie crowns the fence with it, it winded in the garden where the hung veil blows.

Plus also dresses—jewely, gowny things hanging in the pin oak tree Cissie picks from in the morning, picking for days the black cape hung with the black flapping threads Momma used to dance in to dance in. But she does not dance like Momma. When Cissie starts some loopy jig for a boy with half a head for it to chance a leg to look at, even our birding Bingo stops to watch like me instead.

But also there is Momma to watch. Cissie puts the music on and Momma lifts the bedsheets up for foot room and room enough for knees to twitch and rocking hips left gownless in the drifty light the lifted sheet has let in. I do not say, *Did not*. I do not say, *Nome*.

I pull away her sheets from her, from her feet turned out at the foot of her bed—but she does not say, *Orbit*. Cissie does not say, *Orbit*.

The filly hangs from the pin oak tree with still the show of Momma's gowns until there is just the one gown to pick from in the morning. I go out in the morning. Some strange bird sings. I go out with goldenrod poked into my buttonholes to walk beneath the trees with her, the bright sun high by then, with only still the filly hung to ornament the pin oak tree Cissie picked clean in the morning.

It is a yellow morning.

The hems of the drapes in Momma's room blow where we can see outside the house across our yard.

Cissie says, "Say it's when you want to sleep and I'm your bad dream, see."

Cissie's hands are hard and dry and running down

my neck I dream. She says, "Hold still, Orbit."

She says, "Say I am the shadow that you walk on down the road at night, but it is yet so dark at night, you will not think to think of me. You will not remember me. But there will be some dream. Say I am in the garden. Say I am some old yellow sleep come climbing up the stairs at night to walk you to the garden. Come. I walk you to the garden."

I can smell the rain clouds building out above our lake, the long, chuffing thunder come swift to drive us home. I think how we rode home. Sometimes Cissie's skirt rose up and sometimes Cissie's hair rose up and caught between my teeth and in my mouth where I had breathed it. Still no rain fell. Cissie had said when the rain would fall, then there would be no nests of bones the kingbirds make, then there would be no sister, calling from a rocking skiff to swim to her across the lake. I swam to her to: *Orbit*.

We do not turn back.

We go on walking until we cannot see the garden, until I cannot see the lean-to showing blue between the creaking trees I have not shown to Cissie.

The bird we saw in the garden comes scrawing out its strange song it sings for us to follow, so we follow, seeing the bird wait in the trees when we stop to lift the heavy gown to leave the weight of fallen leaves and needled dust we walk through, that Momma's gown gathers up, dragging, as we walk. We walk to a ledge where a brook runs through, where the sun drops sudden through the leaves of the trees like something we have asked for, something we would shy away to make a noise to ask for.

Cissie lies down. When Cissie lies down, through the pearly crown's fishnet veil, I can see the bird shadow sweep across her face.

"I want to fall asleep so long the kingfishers steal my hair," she says.

"My hair is so long," she says.

Cissie spreads her hair beside her for a pillow for my head. She makes a bed of Momma's gown along her I can lie on. Now is no bird nor shadow now, no mark where we have named the trees to see to find our way by—no tailing dog, no broken fence, no way for us to know now if Momma howls nor sings.

"Do you think I'm pretty, Orbit?"

"Yes and no. Sure," I say.

"I think we better go," I say.

"Oh, shut up, Orbit. You could hang yourself at the foot of her bed and Mother wouldn't think twice of it."

Cissie has a beaded purse and in the purse a plastic bottle. She unscrews the top from the bottle and puts the bottle in my hand.

"Try some of this," she says. "It's good for scrapes and bruises."

It is as blue as the lean-to's blue, bluer than a sea blue sea I have not swum in.

"What's it for, Cissie?"

"To make you want nothing. More of it—you want that. But otherwise nothing."

"But why should I want nothing?"

"Oh, never mind, Orbit."

So I take a big sip from it, another sip like Cissie says.

She says to lie here. We have to lie here. The kingfishers, if we are still, will steal our hair to knit the bones to nest upon the water.

Today is not a wind at all even on the water. I know today our lake is bright, so you can see your shadow gone to pieces in the water. Still if ever you swim, your shadow swims with you.

Once a bright leaf falls. Once I saw a silver fish trail me in the water. Even if I swam hard, even if I did not quit, when I quit, I saw the fish beneath me silvering my shadow gone to pieces in the water.

The fish was as quick as my tongue. It was small enough to swallow—small enough to swim inside my mouth if I had let it.

I wish I had let it.

Momma says that, in her mouth, spiders have spun a web and webbed her toes and fingers.

Maybe you also feel it. If it is bright, you see a shadow, even if your eyes are closed, fall across your face. But I think you can feel it. I feel Cissie's shadow, I think, fall across my face. Then I feel Cissie's heart start to pound against my face.

"Open your mouth, Orbit."

In Moon Lake, the catfish grow as big as boys and dogs.

The lake was once a bend in the river.

There is a lake nearby where our father grew up that goes by the name of Reelfoot. Beneath it is a fault called New Madrid, the stress falling on the first syllable, the open *a,* the plea: New *Ma*drid. For days, at the time of the earthquake that formed the lake, the waters of the Mississippi ran backward.

Let me say I stood in our stand of corn, seeing the wind move the drapes out past Mother's window. I heard them; they have those little weights in them that beat a slow, tapping sort of sound against the clapboard. When the wind stopped, the drapes hung flat against our house.

It got to be needles.

She was begging me for it. The morphine we had, the bottle the doctors had given us, was enough to kill off the whole house of us, and the swaybacked mare, too. Mother ranted to get up out of her bed to get up into the closet to it where she had seen me keep it.

I gave her enough to sleep through it, is all, so she would quit begging me for it.

That was all.

It got to be she quit begging me for it, quit begging or sleeping or eating at all, or wanting at all like she used to want to have something cleaned or moved in the room like she used to want, or to be touched. Mother lies there, like she's like now, lying flat the way Mother does now.

I said, "Hold still. You lie here, Orbit."

I held him.

I could see the way we took, the curved mounds the gown had left when we lifted the flounce in the dust and leaves.

I said, "Now we have a secret. Now you know what I am glad of most: that Mother doesn't speak my name."

When I have raked the glass and nails across our road at night, when I have washed our momma's feet and filled the trough where the tadpoles swim and mended with the cast-off hangers Cissie strew beneath the pin oak tree the broken place in the wire fence the wiry coats of the dogs snag on, I ask her.

"Can't we go now?" I ask her. "Haven't I stayed?"

Cissie is with the rabbits down squatting in the yellow dirt. She has dirty knees.

"You know we can't," she says. "What about your mother? We can't just pick up and waltz off to the fair."

But I say, "Cissie."

I had not meant *Cissie*—not thought of her, that she would go.

I say, "I thought me and Bingo might would go down to the fair."

Tonight is just the slough to cross, the stubbled stretch of dusty field I bent my spokes and, days ago, punctured both my tires on. Now is no thrum nor rattle, no swoop I keep my breathing from.

I go by foot, by flattened path. I leave my bike in the garden.

I take my pail, my hollow pole, my chicken necks and fishy eggs the whiskered fish are wise to. The list Cissie makes of things to buy, I take—but I leave Bingo.

There is no sign of Bingo.

At the lake is a new moon, shining. It is best on a night when the moon is thin to lie alone in your metal skiff to listen for your skiff to tick and slur with the swim of the snakes' thick bodies. They are in the deep part you dive into with stones to ride, or some times, by some skinny chance, you find them in the shallows. I pole out from the shallows—past pale frogs squat in the laps of trees I since have grown and done with. Such frogs—some harmless, yippy, simple-sighted house-gyp's easy prey.

It is a hard row open-handed out to reach the deeper water, a clever eye that catches sight, by thin moon, of their mouths. It is the best a boy can hope to see is see inside their mouths. Else there is a place to look where you can see the water welt, which you have got to watch for.

Then you have got to lie down.

You have got to listen.

Listen: I know it is cold down there at night against the water.

Because also, it is August. Also I was dressing, thinking only of the haze of heat that lies on us in August. Still I wait here; you have to wait here. Maybe there is fog here, the thin moon down.

I don't think they hear me.

I have got my chicken neck poked onto my hook I strung from my pole our daddy gave me. Maybe they can smell it. They smell with their tongues.

Do you know there is a good chance that tadpoles see a simpler world than we humans do?

We can see their legs inside them, their pinpricks behind their toes of their tiny ears. Their ears are not like our ears.

A boy can hear the frogs.

But frogs hear only frogs I hear.

The frogs cannot hear Momma. The frogs cannot hear Cissie out singing in the wind at night to lost dogs if they come.

But maybe they won't come. Maybe since I fixed the fence, then it will be just snakes tonight to come into the garden, and garden snakes are garden snakes. They are not like water snakes, which rob the nests the kingbirds make if ever there are calm days and no wind on the water.

Now is not a wind at all to move you on the water.

Do you know where the Pacific is? Because there is a frog I heard of there which lives on some island there which I would like to look at.

It is not like our frogs here. It is very rare, I hear. But I would like to look at it.

I can see the water welt starboard past my metal skiff I kneel up in to paddle. So I cast out, I think to cast out. I have my stone to stone them with if I miss my pail. I have my pail, my good stout lid on it, which Daddy says you have to have if you are ever going to make a nickel at the fair.

But first you have to cast out.

Come on, Orbit.

I bet some egg-sucking snake lives there, where the frogs live out on that island there, and that is why they do it—the little ones.

They are not like our frogs.

They are not like turtles. Their eggs are not thin eggs like Doll's that she leaves out by the road some night for snakes maybe to find some night while we are in the garden.

And they are not like tadpoles. They do not swim. Their legs grow up outside of them, growing in their mother's back—her back as smooth as Doll's smooth back they squat on until the weight of them pocks themselves a place in her that she will have to carry.

I have got to cast out.

They are so near.

But Bingo is not with me. If Bingo does not look for me and Cissie does not look for me, since I have said to Cissie we are going to the fair?

I have got to paddle. But to paddle since I saw them near?

So I have got to lie here.

Maybe they are under here. I am not a scaredy. I am going to lie here. It is safe to lie here. I am sure to lie here that it is safe to lie here, that it is safe to listen at the skiff for the tick, for the slur they

make, the barbed fast boil of the cottonmouths' thick
bodies.

In the morning, I see raincrows cawing in the trees.
I have seven quarters, fourteen dimes, so many nickels
yet to count and dog's tail in my pocket, pool to play
in my pockets, since it is just the rough road nobody
ever comes on much to climb out on from the hollow.

Sometimes if a car goes by, I think, *Is that the car
gone by unlighted, with its engine off if I am in the garden?
Is Bingo in the garden?* I watch for her in trucks gone
by until one truck is a pick-'em-up truck that the
fellows in it turn around and turn back around again
to drive it out ahead of me to wait for me to follow.
The one fellow says, *All be,* and the other one goes,
Shew.

"All be," the one says, "will ye look at them
shoes?"

"Damned if it ain't that scoundrel's boy," the other
goes. "Shew."

"Will ye look at them goddamn shoes?"

I have put my squeaky shoes to ride clean atop my
pail until I near to town.

"How far is it to town?" I ask.

"Fur. Fur enough. Oh, fur."

"What ye got shut in that bucket, boy?"

It is an old pick-'em-up truck with dents and rust
and muddy clumps and cans thrown back in the back

of it, rattling tools and antlers, shot shells, I see, and leafy wads and the misspat spray of tobacco juice but: true. It is a far piece, true, by road or wood for a body to get to town.

"Cottonmouths," I tell them.

"Cottonmouths? Shew."

"Ain't but two kind of snakes he's afraid of. Live ones and dead ones."

"You git back in the back then, boy. Shew."

I put in my lidded pail, my stone for luck I have kicked from home, and before my legs are swung to clear the beaten-up sides of the bed of the truck, we are hell-bent howling down the road run to rut and ruin by the last good trough of rain.

I keep my pail from tipping.

I catch my cap; I dust my shoes.

I am so lucky! By hoof bent and ailing truck, by day and dark, I'll reach there.

What boy is this?

Buhl Parson's boy!

Pray, boy. A peek, boy. What have you got in that bucket?

A hole, ma'am. A dancing toad. A six-legged armadillo.

Come riding, else walking, they come poor of shoe and pocket it is my good luck to fill—prayerful old disheartened hearts one and all for music come, for dancing and the girly sweet of candy in the air. For Clem come, always Clem, and for the carnies barking—*A whale! A whale! The great white Clem!* Harpooned in a covered truck they haul him fifty counties in.

Forty-nine foot long of him!

Nigh on seven tons of him!

None but a shoaty eye to show and nary a tooth nor tongue in him! A marvel! A wonder! An amazement to behold!

Come on, boy! Move on, miss! Come back, boy, he is smooth back here—I will let you hold him.

Yes, but, mister, can you tell me this? Tell me how old Clem is. I want to know how old he is. Is he as old as that turtle is come flippered from the selfsame sea which he has got a glass trough of which we can see him swim in? Is he that old, your Clem? Is he?

Oh, move on. Will ye git on, boy. Go win yerself some gewgaws for your sister from the fair.

Here is what I figure—a quarter and two nickels which I will have to part with once to see Clem at the fair. Before, a peek inside my pail would set you back a nickel, but then was when I went the last with Daddy to the fair. I have seven quarters. Now if I charge a penny, five times is a nickel, so for five times two times, I can see Clem seven times for every ten lids seven times I lift up at the fair.

I put my hand against my throat so I can feel me say it—*Clem, Clem.*

Buhl Parson. Buhl Parson's boy. Old Buhl Parson's boy. Clem.

But by and by, we are bumping past where the road forks for the fair.

I knock my knuckles against the window. The one fellow rides with his head hung back to show the whiskey slugs he takes that his long throat moves to swallow.

"Right-o," he says. "Okeydoke. Hold yer horses, Slim."

The truck shoots out underneath me. Broken jacks and rusty cans, headless screws and socket sets sail, skipping the ribby bed of the truck. I am flopped back, paddling for a hold to grab. I find my feet to stand up, and duck the limbs of roadside trees.

We are going faster. And we are getting farther.

So I have got to figure: tarsals and metatarsals, greensticks, spirals. Tibia, fibula, femur: There are two hundred and some-odd bones in the human body. Of these, I have broken eleven legs, thirteen arms, twenty-two toes and fingers.

I spy a string to make a splint with and slip it in my pocket. But then I see my pail. I see the fellow driving us, still driving us with his elbow bent to stick out his side window. So I figure. I turn my boy's back on them so they can't see me tip my pail, so they cannot see Oscar, so it is just my pail they see

I swing outside the window of the one who goes *shew*.

"Shew," he goes. "Shew, boy."

I let my pail swing in at him, closer every time it takes for him to guess ahead and back again, back to the lucky fib again it has come to me I told him. *Cottonmouths,* I told him; we are proof of it—slung wheel-locked in a dusty skid I tip my cap at the finish of.

"I thank you, sir. And you, sir." I hop down in my shiny shoes, with my turtle worked to my seat of my pants, to march—oh, slippery whelp!—the short piece to the overshot tin trumpet's call to the fair.

Oh, Buhl's boy, Buhl Parson's boy.

So now I have my bucket. I have my yellow house I know, set back from a road I know, and if I walk to the back of the house, I see the rope, the pulley, the open mouth of thick pipe set in the drilled ground.

At the bottom of the pipe is a bucket.

I cannot see it. But I can say that it is filled.

The bucket Orbit leaves in the back of the truck, since I have said so, is empty. It is lidded. But—that drunken night or another, on some female curve or another on some hardscrabble county road—suppose that the bucket tips over. Suppose it is found tipped over.

There is a story I have often heard told in Tuscaloosa. There was a boy in a fishing boat on the lake
near Tuscaloosa. I am not so sure it was August. It
may be later, toward winter, the breeding season, when
the nests are seen to rise in the lake and the eggs, it
is said, of the cottonmouths are moving deep in their
bodies. Onlookers on the banks of the lake claim the
boy fell from the fishing boat. The boat was narrow,
they say, not a deep boat, not a boat you would find
to be hard to rock and, rocking, to get tipped over.

They dragged the lake there. It occurs to me to
wonder why it is they dragged the lake there. Maybe
it is something that must be done, that there is some
sort of decree about, nothing you are left any choice
about, but I am guessing that someone, some family
one, thought it was something that should be done,
that someone ought to take it upon himself to have
the lake be dragged. And when he had, when the lake
was dragged, when the body of the boy was on the
bank you see the snakes sun on there, when it was
seen there, when people gathered there to see it—
the body, the boy it is said to have looked by then to
have rolled down a hill as boys will do, but that this
boy, punctured, spun out of a breeding nest, it is said
that the way this boy looked, it was a long hill he had
rolled down wrapped in barbed wire—then was the
father, I wonder, was the sister, was whoever it was
who decided for the boy, for the son, the brother, that
he ought to be brought out of the lake and seen on
the smooth bank there—were they, even then, that

father, that sister, were they thinking ahead even then to how it might be told again, and knowing that it would be told again, how the story, the spectacle, the outrageous trick by common blood forevermore recast them?

Or before then, I wonder, before that, before the body had been seen at all, before the nets, the slow boat, before it was decided to drag the lake—then—even before then—before it occurred to anyone that someone was going to have to decide to have the lake be dragged, or not—I am not saying yes, or no, only that I wonder—no, that I suspect—hope, I hope I am not alone in this, in thinking that in the decision made there was likely to be, apt to have been, some notion—that in the spectacle of the body, in the freak show of the body, was the promise for them, the endurance for them, of some fresh exile, some uneasy glory.

"Clem?" Cissie says. "You saw Clem? And how is Clem, Orbit?"

I have not got prize one I brought Cissie from the fair. I have not got Oscar, and not my pail I took him in, so now I have to use a pan, which it is just a shallow pan I sneaked out from the kitchen. And the trough is almost empty. In the trough is just a puddle left where the few tadpoles left over swim since Cissie dumped the rest of them, which I will pick up by their tails to count them in the garden. Each by each, I will line them up, snoot to tail in the yellow vein, to fold them into the smooth leaves to bury them out in the garden.

"How come Bingo isn't out digging up the garden?"

"How should I know?" Cissie says. "It isn't me who took her off and left her at the fair."

But I did not leave Bingo. I say, "She did not come."

I am at the kitchen sink to fill the pan I thought to try to sneak into the garden.

"And what if Daddy comes?" Cissie says. "Maybe you think I could borrow your pail to fix him up a chicken."

But there will be no pan she needs and there will be no chicken.

On Momma's head, she rests her hand like there is a hat to keep there, like there is a wind inside the house only she feels come. But this is not the garden. The night wind does not come. The filly does not hang inside to turn above the snapping reach of stray dogs should they come.

I know why they come.

I say it is not for her, but I know why they come.

We light the lights back burning. I fix back the broken place to be again a broken place so when our Bingo comes back home, she can duck into our yard. I leave the windows open so we hear her in our yard.

But how will we hear Oscar? Cissie brings our beds from the garden. Our beans are stripped in the garden. So how can we see Oscar coming slowly should he come?

And Sugar should she come?

You can see the lights all burning. But still the dogs will come. It is still so hot at night that even with our windows closed we can hear them come.

So sometimes they are open.

Sometimes, with our windows closed, you cannot hold your breath enough long enough in Momma's room to stand the smell to sit there thinking why they come. So sometimes they are open.

Sometimes Momma watches me lift the windows open.

Sure—I know there are dogs out there.

I know that, with the windows up, Momma hears the dogs out there fighting for the filly in the yard when dark is come. I lift the windows open. I know dark is come.

I know should our daddy come, then there will be no talking then of sleeping in the one bed Cissie makes of two beds we sleep in in the pantry near to Momma's room.

But there will be the lean-to.

There will be our broken place our Bingo by and by will find, and there will be our Gander still, honking in our yard.

Still, Bingo does not come. I thought with the other dogs surely she would come. "Come. Come."

They said, *Come on, boy. You cain't see from there. Why, it's Parson's boy—old Buhl's boy. It's Orbit.*

They put me up on the bandbox by the stage, where I could see.

I know the girl was watching me. I saw she could see me in the tent light there. I could hear the carnies singing *Clem* out there.

Maybe I am mistaken. It is not unlikely that I am. But I do believe it was August. I am almost sure it was August. It is the order of things I am never quite so sure of myself of. I would say that Orbit went to the fair before we missed Bingo, though, before we went to the lean-to, though—because I remember thinking then, when Orbit had gone to the fair, I remember having to remind myself that it was just so quiet then because my brother had taken our dog with him. Because it was so quiet, you see, and I would have to remind myself that they were going to have to walk, Bingo and my brother—they would have to walk a ways just to get themselves to a place in the road where I know you can hear the fair.

So it would be a while, I knew. It would take those two some walking, I knew, just to get to the goddamn fair. I knew I ought to get myself to where I didn't need to remind myself that it was bound to be quiet —that there were just the two of us, that it was going to be quiet a while because it was just going to be me for a while who moved in the house with Mother.

There was not yet rain then. There was not a sound, I know, of the rain coming down on the roof of our house—because it calmed me, that sound, the sound of the rain on the tin of our roof, so that now, surely I would be certain now to remember that I had heard it. The car for nights we had heard coast by—I didn't hear it at all. It was only, I think, myself I heard, mostly, I think, my feet I heard on the old boards, walking out and into the rooms of our house I heard when it was just the two of us, when Bingo and Orbit were gone.

It is best to keep secrets with the dying, I think. It would be our secret.

I drew the sheet back. I fixed the needle. For weeks, she had begged me for it—to be done with it. And then she stopped begging at all.

I did not rest much. I was waiting for her. I was waiting for some sort of signal from her. The names Mother had I knew of for things I knew fell away. Still I thought there would be some signal, you see; I thought there would be some way for me that Mother would find of asking me, something I could do or say, so that there would be some way to know, so that there would have been some way to think it wasn't me who wanted it, that it wasn't my want at all.

It was quiet; it would be quiet.

It was just me with Mother then—no fathers then, no doctors, no dogs in Tuscaloosa.

I cannot say how many days it was that the other two were gone. I know that the rain came later. The sound of the geese was later, the lake, the lean-to—I think of these as later. I think sometimes that the quiet then, that whatever it was that happened to us happened without our speaking then—that this is why, now—this is what it is now that makes it so hard for me now to remember what happened, to believe that anything happened.

But this is silly.

Orbit was gone, and Bingo was gone, and I was at home with Mother. I stayed by the bed with Mother. I kept the filled syringe in her drawer.

Before we took them away from her, Mother kept her cigarettes on the nightstand that stood beside her bed for all the nights of all the days I myself could speak of. It was the one thing she seemed to remember, the one thing Mother insisted on—on having one of her hands free to reach across the bedsheets with to pick up one of her cigarettes that we had long since decided she had had enough chances by then to get burned up in bed with, and us in bed with.

But she would reach for them. She would feel around on her nightstand for them and bring her hand up close to her mouth, with her mouth a rounded shape she made as though she was really smoking, as though she were somebody my age then practicing for smoking. For all the times I sat there and saw Mother reach for a cigarette, still when it was quiet like that, when we were alone in the house like that, I would catch myself thinking that Mother had reached for me.

There was a restlessness in me.

It is hard for me to explain it. The weeks passed, the days. Years pass. Years pass. There are houses. Favorite dogs have died.

I cannot explain it.

A redbird flies at the windowpane. A river turns tail on the sea.

The shadows made by the pin oak tree pooled on Mother's bedsheets. She tried to kick them off, to sweep them off with the backs of her hands, to go out. She was always wanting to go out. When the last of the shadows left the room, the sun had dropped over the sea.

That was when she would go out, when she had gone out—before then, before our father left. I had heard the bones of her hips crimped against the kitchen counter. She was peeling something, washing. Whatever it was, she put down. She went out.

She used to let us go with her.

There were geese those years I know Mother loved, and the pelicans that followed the river. I know Mother loved the river.

We were walking with her on the levee one day. We were behind her. Her hands reached behind her to stop us. We were to go back. There was something she had left in the oven for us that we were to eat for dinner.

We listened for her. We left the porch light on. Orbit dropped marbles in an empty can he set inside the door of our room and, from the can, walked a string from our room down the hall to wrap around the knob of the door so that when she came back, we heard her.

There were times we did not hear her. We popped the screen from our window. The tree frogs had started to call. The call grew louder, quickened toward dark. Whippoorwills walked the road till dark, calling themselves out slowly.

Did you think we would follow, Mother?

We lay on our beds by the window, our pillows doubled beneath us, to see across the field. Our field was silted. Our potatoes were fists in the ground we tilled—held out, rooting.

We grew restless.

We sang.

A horse and a flea and three blind mice, sitting on a tombstone shooting dice. Horse jumped off, fell on the flea. Oops! said the flea. There's a horse on me!

Boom boom. Boom boom.

We never followed her to the river. Our father was in his room. We kept having to remind ourselves that our father was in his room—that we should be quiet, that it would be dark before Mother came back, because it was a ways to the river and back. We would fill a plate for her and leave it to warm in the oven for her so that she would eat some dinner.

And then this stopped also.

The fields were burning. It was the time of the year our father went out among the other fathers to burn the grass in the fields.

Our field was burning. We spelled one another at the windowsill. We could smell the grass still burning. The flames were brief, guttering birds.

We saw her.

She was growing old.

We saw the light of her cigarette drop at her feet from our window.

Then we did not see her. We did not think we could see her.

We called out. We did not think to call out. Ash rose to our mouths in the field.

I did not dawdle. Cissie says I dawdled there, but I did not dawdle. It is just a long way there. I came quick.

I did not have shoes. I did not have Bingo with me going there or coming back, and coming back I came by foot and I did not have shoes. I did not have Oscar, not my pail to bring him in and not my pail to rest on turned up, tired, by the road. And it is such a rough road. But I came quick. I came in my sock feet. I had swapped my shoes.

I swapped them at the tent. Also all my coins I had which I had not yet parted with—I swapped them at the tent.

My shoes,
my coins,
my lidded pail,
my fishy eggs,
my chicken necks,
my stone I kicked for luck from home,
my store list Cissie gave me—

lost, and worst of all is Oscar lost, and worse by far is Bingo lost, and also figure tadpoles lost, folded in the yellow leaves since I left through the field.

There is always Clem there. The Ferris wheel was broken. But there is always Clem there, and the turtle which swims in the tank.

The tent was flapping. I had on my shoes.

"First off," the boy said, "you got to remove them shoes."

I took out my coins I had.

I took off my shoes.

They smelled like Daddy. The ticket booth smelled like Daddy. Where I touched my shoes and the ticket booth, I smelled him on my hands.

· · ·

I had smelled the roe, too, and the chicken necks when morning came, the morning I went to the fair. My pail was empty. I knelt in my skiff to paddle. I had to paddle with my hands. My hands were rotty. First I had the necks to lob and the bright eggs of the fish to lob where the lake is deep where the catfish swim, so that when I got to the shallows, when I got to the bank of the lake, I could haul my skiff up away from the lake and rinse it out with my empty pail and tip it up so if the rain should fall, the snakes would not swim in it.

The catfish had to swim up from the bottom.

I threw the eggs and the chicken necks as far away from my metal skiff as I could make them go. But I could still see the fish swimming. Even the eggs they swam for. The eggs were so small.

The snakes came and went for the eggs, but the snakes were small also. The fish were as big as dogs. I saw them swimming. I threw the fish eggs one by one, but once I threw a bunch at once so the fish would fight for them.

But I did not want to see the fish.

I did not want them bumping me.

I did not want to feel their whiskers pulling past my arms.

The boy was putting on my shoes. The boy was just a tall boy, stepped up taller in the ticket booth.

He was not an older boy much by far than me. When he walked, my shoes made squeaking sounds like the sounds they made on me. My coins wore songs in his pockets.

I stepped up with the boy in the ticket booth. There was a mark on the wall of the booth that even tipped up on my toes I could not reach with my head.

"Uh-oh," the boy said.

I was too small, he said.

I had seen my daddy—he had walked into the tent.

The men inside the tent were clapping. There was music when the clapping stopped. But I was still not tall enough. Even tipped up on my toes, I was not yea tall as that for the boy to let me in.

My hands were in my pockets. I could not make a run for the tent because my hands were in my pockets. I had to keep them in my pockets.

I listened for him. If I listened hard enough and if I stayed still long enough, I heard Oscar's neck come out and sometimes, too, his feet came out and I would feel him walking on my legs between my pockets.

I had heard him, on the bank of the lake, in the weeds as soon as the sun came up. I had pulled my skiff up. I had my lidded pail. Oscar's feet made slow scraping sounds when I put him in my pail.

. . .

The boy had a scar on his forehead.

I thought the boy had sisters.

I thought the boy had a stone to kick, or to keep with his hands in his pockets. But he did not have sisters. I gave him my store list Cissie wrote, since he did not have sisters. But he did not have pockets.

I thought all boys had pockets.

I thought all boys had sisters, girls to carve their names in trees and in the shells of turtles boys can carry by their pockets.

"How old did you say your sister was?"

How old do you think Oscar is? How old are you, Cissie?

I swapped my shoes, my lidded pail, my Oscar who I held up in my pants between my pockets. I swapped until the boy in the ticket booth promised to let me in.

It was dark almost inside the tent when I first went in. The stage was empty. The men inside stopped talking. I could not see them yet, coming into the dark from the bright outside, but they saw me. They said, "It's Buhl's boy. Why, Parson's boy. Hey, Orbit."

They smelled like piss and horses. They lifted me up on the bandbox so I could almost see. But I did not see Daddy. I was on the bandbox, sitting, seeing over the hats of the men, but I could not see Daddy.

"Somebody tell Parson that his boy has found him here."

But I could not hear Daddy.

On my hands, I could smell my shoes. I heard the thick flaps of the tent beat in the wind outside the tent and the boy walking out in the wind outside. I could hear my shoes. It was just the trees I heard and the wind that beat the flaps of the tent and the squeaking steps my shoes made and then the music started. It was just the one light when the music started. The light shined down along her. She had feathers in her hair, the girl, that flew out when she danced. She had a jerky way of dancing, a tooth that as she danced I saw her loosen with her tongue.

"Quit that," Cissie says. "What is it now, Orbit?"

I pull the porch light on.

I say, "Oscar will not come tonight. Will he, Cissie? And Daddy not the next night?"

Not even if we hear the cars go quiet past out there. You cannot see the trees out there. Tonight the trees are quiet.

Even if that boy left him there to find his own way home from the fair, still there would be the road to cross, the slough, the stubbled field to cross—so even if Oscar came on, even if Oscar did not stop, it would be high time by then, by the time we maybe saw him, to polish our swapped shoes again to be on our way from home by then to see Clem at the fair.

There is not a leaf that turns. There is not a drop

that falls. There are not the trees to see until the bright heat lights them.

"Is that all, then?" Cissie says. "That's what you wanted to ask me?"

We leave the porch light burning.

Momma is in her room.

We try to go how Momma went when Momma could leave her room. We walk along the dirt road that quits against the paved road the river runs on beside of and takes the boats to sea. Ours is just a small boat. It is just a lake boat. It is not a boat to ride the river out to sea in.

The river moves fast.

It sweeps beneath the limbs of the trees that bend along the broken bank.

The rain clouds stay at the river, at the crooked lake the river left. *Go on.*

The pelicans go on.

We do not turn back. We go on walking down, catching onto the limbs of the trees to reach the high wall of the barge, the low rail of the sloping deck we use the chains to climb to. The chains come up from the river. We swing our feet up over them to monkey up the slope to the barge, the mud of our shoes dropping past into the passing river.

I say, "Be careful, Cissie."

The river goes to sea. The sea ourselves we have

not seen nor had the taste nor smell of. We lie on our backs on the deck of the barge. We lie so our heads hang away from the barge, listening to the river.

Say the river turns back.

"I saw a girl at the fair," I say. "Her hair was kinked and yellow. It was not like your hair. I did not want to touch her hair."

My hands were dirty. My hands smelled like Oscar smelled and my hands smelled like Daddy—like the shoes I wore to the ticket booth, the eggs I threw to the whiskered fish, the necks I threw so I could flip the skiff so the snakes would not swim in it.

She danced. The men were hooting. They were calling for the next girl, calling for something else. She took her top off, her thin brassiere. She took her time with her panties, tugging till they fell down, till they were on the floor. Then she quit dancing. She got down into the webby chair folded out in the swinging light. She let her legs drop open. She pushed the eggs up into her—three, I counted. Four. Maybe I lost count of them.

Maybe they were Doll's thin eggs.

Maybe they were the kingbird's eggs, crowning in the gash she dropped her legs apart to show us. She did not want to show us. She popped them out again. I saw her watching. I saw she could see me in the tent light there. She lobbed the eggs over the hats of the men. But I did not want to catch the eggs. I did not want to touch her skin, and not the small eggs that broke and left in her no shell I saw, no shut place she could open.

Say the river turns back.

Say the river turns back, sucking at the sea to turn, will the pelicans turn back also, Cissie? Will the salted fish turn back when the sea has turned back to run back into the sea itself in the turning river?

Go on. Our lake is our lake. Our barge is chained here. Go on.

The fair stays here for twelve days. Then is yet the next town I can think of that it goes to. Then the fair stays eight days. Then figure for the next small town as small by far as our small town, it stays for maybe ten days. I cannot figure. Maybe I lost count of them. I counted nine and seven—the nine eggs going into her, the seven coming out.

Plus there is this also—also to think how many times to figure in a fair night they can fill the tent to do it. It is not a big tent. And where they find the eggs she keeps, plenty more would come. Twelve, say, eight days, ten days spent in Little Crab, plus maybe days in towns to go I have not even thought of. So say another two towns. Say she does it twice a night, since maybe they won't wait for her to let the tent get filled. She is seventeen, say, or maybe she is twenty.

Maybe it is nothing you can start before you're twenty. So maybe she is twenty. Couldn't she be twenty?

Maybe it is not a redbird. It could be a kingfisher bird. Couldn't it, Cissie? Because don't the kingfisher birds steal bones to knit them on the water?

The bones could be our Bingo's bones, the small bones of the birds she kills, the bones of Momma's fingers.

Couldn't they, Cissie?

Because maybe it is not a redbird.

Maybe it is a kingfisher bird.

Maybe it flies at the windowpane because kingfisher birds need bones and hair and there are the bones of Momma's hands and the hair that falls from Momma's head and the hair that falls from your own head and from my head also.

And we have bones also.

Her shoes were dirty. Momma's skirt of her dress was dirty. I felt the cool where the skirt of her dress, where the cloth of her skirt, doubled back, dried from the river still. Our mouths were burning. The fireflies were burning.

.   .   .

"There, now," Cissie says.

"Let's go now," Cissie says. "Hum up, Orbit."

The boats are moving. The lamplights are on. But we are not moving. We are not moving. Our beds are one bed. Our lake is our lake. Our barge is chained here. Go on. She is here with us now. She will die with us. Go on.

The bird came back when Orbit came back. I heard it hitting at the windowpane again.

It kept on at it. For a time I could not see it. I thought at first it was mud Orbit threw, but there was no mud to throw, no rain yet to pock the dust to clop against the windowpane so that I would lean across her bed and say through the window, *Orbit? What is it now, Orbit?*

But he did not throw it.

He was working at his tree.

His ax made hammering sounds working at his tree. The blade was shiny. The light that fell from Mother's room, Orbit chopped the tree by. There were pieces chipped of the bark of the tree and of the pale wood of the tree scattered in Orbit's shadow as if it were not his shadow but a still pond by some accident he had stepped in there.

He swung the ax back. He had choked up on the handle. I saw it slipping in his hands. The window sweated. I let it close then.

I saw the bird swoop down then from where it sat in the pin oak tree, where the filly shook in the pin oak tree when the iron head of the ax homed, and so I pushed it up again, the window, the shadow of the window sash lifting on my brother's back—and the bird banked.

It was a redbird. I saw that it was a redbird. It was common.

I pushed the window open enough to lean out past the windowsill to be heard above the chuck of the ax. I saw he had not eaten. I saw the plate I had brought to him gathering wood chips still. Orbit's shirt hung down from the waist of his jeans for a rag to keep to wipe his hands and the shadow had lifted off his back and gone off into the leaves of the tree and I leaned out.

"Hold out your hands for me," I said. "Let me see your hands."

I saw his shirt was stained and wadded. He kept his back to me. He went on with the ax.

I said, "Stop it. You've got to stop it."

I said, "You ought to come inside."

But I could not stop him. Even when the tree was down, even with the filly down, dragged away from the pin oak tree, I tried to tell my brother that our Bingo would not come.

But I could not stop him.

I could not stop any of it.

I knew she would not come.

Oh, to be a junkyard dog and run the woods with Daddy!

Gander knocks his beak on our door at night. I keep my vole in my pocket.

I say, "Lookit, Cissie."

I take my hammer.

It is Daddy's hammer.

It is my vole I found. It is in my pocket.

"Lookit, Cissie."

I put my vole on the porch step.

She says, "Stop it, Orbit."

But I do not stop it. I do not stop it. I go on hitting. I hit it on his head.

I was peeling potatoes.

In the sink, the mounding strips of skin gave off the smell of turned earth. Everything had stopped growing. The fireflies lay in the field.

I saw Orbit walking between them in his sock feet in the field.

He was walking to reach the place in the fence he had mended before he left for the fair—he had forgotten. I could see that he had forgotten. His hands were empty. I saw that his cap was frayed.

I peeled all we had of potatoes.

I didn't suppose Orbit had eaten much in however many days it had been, and it had been a ways, I knew. It had taken my brother some walking, I knew, to get back home from the fair.

I boiled the potatoes and poured off the water and added what we had of milk. We had a good dollop of butter. I let it melt some. I used two colors of pepper. I salted the potatoes in a metal pot and mashed them together with the tines of a fork and spooned them into a casserole.

Orbit was burying tadpoles. I was sorry about the tadpoles.

I listened outside the door of the room when he went in to talk to Mother. He told her about the tadpoles, about Clem he had seen and the girl at the fair, about how he thought he'd seen Daddy.

He didn't say a thing about Bingo.

He fixed the fence back. I mean that he pulled it apart again so that Bingo could get back through.

He got the ax out.

It was almost dark when he started. He kept at it, working into the next day and on into the next dark. I carried a big plateful of potatoes to him and set the plate down in the path in the yard beneath the crooked limb of the tree Mother used to read in.

She read limericks. She wore knee-highs.

I closed her mouth some. A tooth had abscessed. The side of her face had swelled.

The rope I used was rotty and thick and there was the hanging weight of it, I said the waiting hang of it. When I went out on the limb of the tree I could see our momma's bedroom from, I saw that the knife blade bent and caught with never so little a nick in the rope I had lobbed across the limb of the tree I had climbed the tree to saw through.

So Momma said to me, "Orbit, so why don't you cut it down?"

So I cut the damn thing down.

I found the ax our daddy used, which I had seen him do it.

After the tree was well and down, it was easy with even a flimsy knife to cut down past the hide of her into the long neck of her, the blade going quick along and smooth behind the soft muzzle even Bingo had fought to get at, that I had seen her jumping with the other dogs to get at. The muzzle was torn from them and hard-blooded and soft-haired still to want to kiss, but I did not stop to kiss it. It was near to yard dark and soon to watch the darkened woods, I would see the dogs.

So I went quick.

I had not thought to think it yet that she said my name: Orbit.

So, Orbit, so why don't you go ahead and cut the damn thing down?

But I had not thought, *Orbit*.

I was thinking of the filly still and the knife blade pulling deep in her and the dark shapes of the dogs I saw bunch up in the field. The light from Momma's window fell bright before the field. It was all the light I worked by. I worked to get the hide free the way once Daddy showed me. First you put her head back. I had put her head back. At first the knife went smooth. It was how he had showed me. At first the knife went smooth the way he had showed me down the front of her, smooth all down the neck of her. It was just a knife I had I sneaked out from the kitchen with and then the light to work by, down by night from Momma's room.

I heard her name me in her room.

It was just the one time. I only heard her one time.

At first the knife went smooth.

We passed the barn; the slough was dry; the lake was left by a river. The lake was dropping. Where the skiff had scraped on the bank of the lake, the paint was flecked and silver.

I did not know why we had come there. I remember the snakes were blind. The skins my brother had found in the woods the snakes by then had begun to shed, and a turtle—Vernon, I remember—and chicken necks, and the rhinestone shoe he had found of Mother's

that had not been chewed or planted; he brought tadpoles, I remember, a poke of frogs—a damp stash he
had gigged in the trees—a flat stone, a kitchen knife,
a lamplight, though the sun was high, though the
moon would rise behind us.

Our house lay bright behind us. We paddled out
with our hands. He threw a frog, a chicken neck. He
threw an old bone from the garden.

We waited.

I didn't know what we were waiting for.

We were quiet.

I did not know why we were quiet.

The lake slapped at our skiff underneath us. I
started to sing. Of the cranes in the trees I sang of,
and of the pelicans I sang of, no cry came.

I sang, *Oh, what a bird is the pelican! His beak can
hold more than his belly can!*

But Orbit didn't want me to sing. We were waiting
for the moon, I thought, for the sun to fluke in the
sea, I thought. I thought he would tip us over. He
threw great wads of tadpoles out and the rhinestone
shoe of our mother's out and our Vernon gone scudding
out in a slapping rain of frogs.

There was something he was trying to show me.
He kept stepping up onto the thwarts of the skiff to
look for it to show me. But whatever it was was not
out there, or he could not see it out there, and Orbit
started to scream at me that I wasn't really trying, I
wasn't really looking, but he never did say what to
look for, see; I never really knew what it was he had

brought me out in the skiff on the lake he had wanted so much to show me.

That was August. It must have been August.

Because I remember Orbit saying to me that the snakes were blind. I know that it is dog days, that dog days are August, that these are the days the skins lift away and the snakes themselves go blind.

Some days the crows are blue if the sun is yellow. The lean-to is blue all days. The weeds are going yellow. Tomorrow if the leaves are green, the next day the leaves are red if they are not yellow.

The girl's hair was blue, then yellow. I did not want to touch her hair.

The redbird was a redbird before I touched the redbird. After, its neck was broken.

I chopped the pin oak down.

I should not have done it.

A tadpole's legs are dark inside, as small inside the skin to cut as when a fly is yellow. I did not want to see the flies. First a fly is yellow. Then are yet the legs to grow, the thin wings and the eyes to grow, though first by night by Momma's room I chopped the pin oak down. I know our momma saw me chop the pin oak down.

Here is what I figure:

But I cannot figure.

Figure there are flies inside.

I pulled the flap back. I had to light a light inside.

Inside the filly are flies inside and in our house also. Also in Bingo worms inside and in our house also.

Inside the snakes are fishy eggs and maybe frogs also, and in the fish also.

Inside the frogs are flies inside and in the filly also, in maybe Bingo also. Maybe fishhooks also.

In the whiskered fish are fishhooks and maybe ducks also. Maybe Vernon also.

There could be a dog.

Then if me and Cissie dove and held our stones and sank with them until we sank to the bottom of the lake and we lay on our backs on the bottom of the lake with our stones on top to hold us, we would hear our dog.

Because I bet she is digging.

We would hear Bingo digging. Because she is just our dog.

Our Oscar put his flap down and walked between my pockets. True:

But I cannot figure *true*.

The pin oak tree is down. The filly, I dragged to the lean-to. It is my lean-to, true. It is my vole I found. It is in my pocket.

If the vole is my vole, is its head mine also? Is it my head also?

Once it was the vole's sharp head. But if the vole is not now, if it was and is not now, its head is only mine now, its feet, its tail mine also.

My broken head,
my feathered neck,
my ropy tail my daddy cut—
mine—
my muzzle also,
my long toes mine,
my yellow eyes,
my bones of Momma's fingers mine.
She will be mine also.

One Mississippi, I count, *two,* to know the seconds by. I think she is not breathing. I try to keep from breathing. But sometimes we breathe.

Her mouth is open. I thought Momma sings. But Momma does not sing, I know. There is no such song she sings that only she can hear, I know.

I take my time some. I wash my finger. I put it in her mouth.

One-five-zero, zero-zero-zero-zero—I cannot remember the zeros it should be—the toothless years the turtles pass. But a tongue, I know the turtles have, a toothless frog a tongue, too, else it would not sing. Else you would not hear it sing.

It is getting looser. I work it with my finger some—a sharp tooth, Momma's dog's tooth.

A goose's tooth, you cannot pull, though Gander knocks at the door at night, though maybe you could pull his tongue to quiet down the yard at night—if you broke his neck first. If you had a pliers.

They are Daddy's pliers.

I work the gum up. I shut the curtains. I pull the window closed.

Listen: Between day and dark, you hear them. With the breath I breathed in Momma's room between her breaths, you hear them.

But the frogs are not calling me.

"Open your mouth, Momma. Open your mouth, Momma."

I thought they were calling me.

But they are not calling me.

They are calling Momma.

Come.

The trees are green still. The cows can be heard feeding. I will keep quite near.

Only come, if you will, from the dirt road that ends, if you wish, at the paved road. Where there is dirt, the path will have been worn smooth. Where saw grass, the blades are broken.

Cross the slough, the levee. I will not be far from you. The way is perfectly clear.

From the levee, you will see a high red bank gouged by the flow of a river. True: Perhaps there is no river.

Perhaps the almanac is right: There will be no river this year.

But the road—there will be the road, yes. The

arroyo, yes. Some truck stop, some Sears. Some fair-grounded border town of tooled belts and Kewpie dolls, dirty-shirt dog shows, souvenir spoons.

Remember he kept a rabbit's foot saved frozen from the garden. Remember a vole in his pocket.

The doors, I left both open—her door and our door.

There was something Orbit wanted to show me. He kept bumping around in the hall for me, to wait for me, to show me. I put my shoes on. The sun was dropping. Mud swallows sang in the eaves. We crossed the yard, the garden, stepping over the boughs of the pin oak tree.

"What is it, Orbit?"

We were marching. We crossed the hidden field. The geese were flying so high above the field, I could hardly hear them. I could not see them. I looked to see over the trees as we went, thinking that I would see them.

We walked on. The path we walked, I could not see myself to follow. Still I followed. The shade was spotty when we reached the trees. I saw a swatch of something blue showing between the trees.

"This is where I come to think," Orbit said.

I saw he had made a lean-to with a tarpaulin in the trees.

"You brought me out here to tell me that? That's what you had to show me?"

.   .   .

No rain falls. No birds swift past. On the bank of the lake is a shallow skiff the riverbend has come to. The river is quite near. The wide boats going slow to sea, you can see from Tuscaloosa.

Tuscaloosa is a good town. There are doctors in Tuscaloosa. No guns, no books, no telephones. But a river—yes. A yellow house, a lake near Tuscaloosa.

The lake is deep, the river. The door to the house is open. Inside the door is a woman's purse. Inside the purse is a pair of gloves. The purse is open. The door is open.

In my mind is an empty room Mother walks into when I speak.

But this is silly.

I sat on my hands in the parlor. I closed the window. I drew the curtains.

Listen to me, Orbit. It was not the sea we heard. It was not Ohio.

It is just a sound I like to hear, the name Ohio.

He said, "Come on, Cissie."

I saw the bird first—it was a redbird. It hung from its feet from a string from a limb the tarpaulin was lashed to.

Orbit folded the flap of the tarpaulin back. There were rows. At the mouth were the rabbits he had brought from the garden whose necks you can break with your thumb. We stepped over the rabbits to step inside—we had to light a light to see. I was too tall to stand inside.

He said, "Close your eyes, Cissie. Open your eyes, Cissie."

A blue wall hung with a gaggle of frogs—pinned, quartered. A yellow cat. A turtle—the beaked neck of a turtle, the dark shards of shell. Orbit had teeth in his pocket. He had a pitchfork, looped with snakes skinned from behind their angled heads, and mice— pink, puny, hairless things Orbit had driven the pitch- fork through, that you could see the prongs of the pitchfork through.

"This is where you come to think?" I said. "You brought me out here to tell me that?"

There was a pin oak tree in our yard. In the tree was a crooked limb—

What of it?

She read limericks; she wore knee-highs.

The yellow cat is a yellow cat.

The blacktop runs beside the river, to sand against the sea.

What of it?

Orbit pulled away the filly's hide, the slab of her rib with the toe of his shoe. He nudged her open.

The way is easy to see—to see her, to word her, to be shut of her. I cannot get shut of her.

Come. There will be a road, an airport. There are lights so bright at airports, you can hear them burning.

Come. Forget about Ohio. The salt bluffs, the sea.

The door is open.

We may go now.

You may leave us.

I drew the sheet back. Needles, implements, morphine, salve. It would have to be needles—the body seen, the witnessed skin. The light grayed, blanched her. Mother's skin grew weak, and pulled away.

Mother, please.

I love you, Mother.

A signal, a word. If she spoke, I did not hear her. Maybe she asked for water. Maybe a light was on.

I drew the sheet back. Her gown was twisted. No rain came, no father. When the rain came, it stayed, the wind, the no-time of waiting through—the dry, disordered days, dog days, days of heat and of the wild cry of geese faintly above the fields and in the dusking garden.

She is years dead. She is dying. I am in some airport.

Everywhere, even where there are no paved roads, still there will be an airport—a strip to portage to, pebbled or clayed, what have you, beaten grass swept of light.

The light is leaving our windows. The Naugahyde booths are dream. I draw her gown back. Our mouths are open.

No birdsong, Mother? No silver fish?

Very well, then. Very well, then.

I fixed the needle.

No fathers then, no doctors, no dogs in Tuscaloosa.

There was nothing I could do for her, nothing I
could not do to her. I rouged her cheeks, teased her
hair. I harvested beets from the garden.

Go on. Go on. There is not a place in you I will
not work into. I work apart bone.

The bland root of me swam between her bones.

The fields are planted. The door is open. The trees
are green still. Go on.

I cannot remember you.

I unremember you.

For years I do not dream of you.

Go on. I give back nothing.

The weeks, the months, they gave me something
to do with myself. I had a sense I liked of myself—
that I was needed, that there was a great givingness
in me, a patient, damaged, holy sort of hardheaded
love in me. Love. Say love. That I waited, say, since
I waited—not to say or have it be said of me that what
I did I did because there was not patience enough in
me, enough faith, love, talk in me, that what I did I
did because there was such a rush in me—there was a
great hurry in me.

Come. Quickly. Come. The lights are burning.
You can hear the lights still burning. I can conjure
up a dream for us, the dopplered wheeze of an engine,
a tire song on a paved road—

But this is easy. To conjure a dream is easy.

To upstage the dead is easy.

I take; I give back nothing. I have had my children scraped from me—accidents of fucking.

No wide swim, no brackish suck.

But the reamed cunt, the scoured earth. The Buick in flames on the highway. The breakfasts, the tea.

Love. Say love. Say something, anything more— that you are sick, or lonely, some wild boy gone to seed one night, some buckaroo I loved one night farmed apart on scag one night, one night when I was twenty. That you are oceans to cross from home, let us say. Or nothing—let us say almost nothing.

In my hands are the hands of your mother.

Let us go now. She may leave us.

Look, you. You, newborn.

Has there been no dream we meet in? No Naugahyde booth we meet in in no tawdry airport bar?

Here's to you, love. And to you, my sweet.

The fields are burning. So, go. Go on, go on. Run tell the doctor, the children, the schools. A signal, a word. Only whisper. Light out. Winter wheat, corn counties. Cave Hill, Carthage. Caspian, Ocoee, Reelfoot, Sargasso.

There is always the next place to go to get to to light out of.

The road lapses. Snow falls—schools close, dog tracks, airports.

There will be some airport.

From the soft palm, the girth of tumor in her— let me say—let it be said of us—of myself and of my mother said—in a Naugahyde booth, in a makeshift bar, in the yellow heat of airports said—some lesser god from the greening rift—beaded, slicked, a pale sheen, a long cock broke to probe me.

Newborn, adieu. Asante.

To you, lad. And to you, my sweet. May we have a good long romp of it. For who will love what we love?

What bright house?

What reading tree?

Who will love our dead for us, the wormy dog at our feet at night, the harpooned corpse of a baleen whale we walk a day to see?

I could not hear her. I saw her talking. Mother for hours made sounds with her mouth in a voice not as loud as breathing. I leaned my head close. I felt her breathing. She was saying thank you. All along, she was saying thank you. Mother was saying thank you.

After all the months of it, the careful doses of morphine, the dressings, the scarves? The Popsicles and floating pears, swabbed teeth, open sores, bludgeoning heat, neighbors, neighbors—for this she thanks me? She dares to thank me?

The long box we build for her, we break her bones to lie in.

Mother kept a cot at the foot of her bed certain nights I slept in. I was sleeping. When I waked up, I found her dead. I pulled the drapes shut. I closed her mouth some. I knew to close her eyes. I left them open. I untied the scarf I had found to use to tie her foot to the bed with. I had taped a needle to a vein in her foot. I took it out. I got the sheet off. I took the catheter out. She had bled from her mouth. I wet a washrag. I took her gown off. Her gown was blooded. I took her pillow. The blood was dry. I wiped her mouth off. I rinsed the washrag. I wiped her neck some. I wiped her shoulder. We had a big barrel we burned in. I burned the gown, the pillow sack. I burned the washrag. I got her arms straight. I turned her feet in. I got her rings off.

We put on lipstick. We put her rings on.

Day came. Men came. Rain.

We sat for the men with our hands in our laps with all that was ours in the parlor.

winter bodies

There is a poisoned mouse in the corner, under the TV stand. There are scarves on the bureau, implements, needles, salve. She is growing thinner. Even her slippers she cannot keep on. There is the TV, the lamp in the room, the things they can see by the light in the room, one another— otherwise, they see nothing. They keep the passing days in mind, inasmuch as they keep the days in mind, by the curtains, drawn, by the door, pulled to—the inevitable flaws, the incisions of light. At night, if they wake, as they often do, the light pales to a humming fluorescence.

She looks up at him from the bed. He has combed his hair back. He carries a picture of her in his wallet.

"What else do you love?" she asks him.

"Nothing."

"Not the wind?" she says.

"Nothing."

He carries a bowl of water to her, a razor, folds the sheet away from her, puts the lamp at the foot of their bed. He begins with the few hairs he has seen on the tops of her toes, the tops of her feet, the hollows she has always missed by the knob of the bone of her ankle. She falls to sleep. He works up her—her shin, nicked, dented, the darker skin of her knee. He slips his hand behind her knee, lifts to bend her leg up, then kneels on the bed between her legs. He shaves swaths in the hair on the backs of her legs. The TV is on. The fine coat of her belly, he shaves. There are tiny hairs on her breasts he shaves, on her shoulders. He goes over her elbows, the backs of her hands, stands up, straightens her legs. He picks the lamp up from the foot of the bed, props it against the pillow.

Then he moves off. He unscrews the handle of the razor, lifts the used blade away from the head. He runs water, holds the razor's head under the water—his hands pale, healed, this boy's. The hair of her hands and her shoulders, some few caught hairs of each place he has shaved, catch against the scoop of the sink or wash off into the pipe of the sink in the running water. There are no surprises. There is a used-blade slot. Probably you cannot hear it—the sound the blade makes in the wall when it drops. Still, you might listen for it. He listens for it. He picks up a pair of scissors that rust in the steady leak of the faucet. He carries these back to the bed.

Oh, the body—the tracks, the lesions, the pumiced knees.

Her lips, her throat, her eyebrows, he shaves. His cock gets hard as he shaves her. He straddles her, leaning over her body. He cuts away her hair with the scissors he has found, close against her skull. His hands are aching. Her hair is heaped on the carpet. He leaves it for the mice on the carpet. He thinks of Tucumcari, of the room they slept in there. Streets, he remembers, and weather. He snips her eyelashes—slowly now, quietly—as though she will never know.

delicious

I did doubles, since I was the new girl. The old girls were strictly evenings. They were Frenchies. Your Frenchies never will work lunch.

I was doubling, the day I'm talking about. The place was empty. I'd gotten slammed, but the crowd cleared out. You get your delinquent diners, sure, but this day the floor cleared out.

I checked the walk-in. I switched off the pot of coffee. Punched out. It's a feeling—punching out.

But then the old stick started coughing.

The owner was gone and the head chef was gone and the old guy had gotten his own menu because the hostess had punched out early. It was hours before the Frenchies would come. Let's face it, I'm gonna tell the old stick to get lost.

For starters, he sat at a six-top. There were two-tops all over the place. But the guy had to sit at a six-top. He was moving stuff around on the table.

"You expecting somebody else?" I said.

"I believe I'll have Alfredo," he said. "Yes. How is your Alfredo?"

"Listen," I started to tell the guy.

"Or snapper. I haven't had the snapper," he said. "But, oh, now. Wait, now. I suppose snapper has those bones. I'm not supposed to have bones," he said. "Something soft," he said, "not too spicy."

"Listen a minute," I said to the guy. "Have you noticed the time lately? 'Cause I already worked the lunch shift."

"Lunch?" he said.

"It's a quarter to four."

The guy tipped up his wristwatch.

"I've got to get back for dinner," I said. No over-time, etc. I mentioned the Frenchies and all.

"Frenchies?" he said.

"Sure," I said.

"*Au bon pain*," says the old guy.

Au bon pain, my ass, say I. I don't speak French. The Frenchies come in and speak French and I don't know a thing they say.

"I'm Swiss myself," said the old guy. He put his hand out for me to shake it.

I didn't get much of a look at the hand. His finger bent into my palm—what was left of his finger did. It was stubbed, blunt where the bump of a knuckle would be. The tip was silky. It was cool. I thought of the bones the boys threw in the bin outside the kitchen door. They were veiny, hacked-off shanks, balls of the balls and sockets. It moved, the finger, the stub of it, pushing around in my palm. I pulled my hand back. He held it.

"Oh, look," he said, "marsala. I adore a good marsala."

I pulled my hand back. I grabbed the menu. I tried to be French about it.

"And wine," he said. "May I see the wine list?"

"We don't have one," I lied.

He tugged off his jacket. A bunch of fat veins popped up in his arms. It was the only thing fat that was on him.

"Something dry, then. Not red," he said. "I can't possibly have the red," he said. "Something French, though. You know. Something oaky."

"Oaky," I said.

"And osso buco."

"I thought you said marsala," I said.

I could smell him. He smelled like something cooking—something sort of sweet to me, cooling. But I saw his skin looked grungy. He didn't look a bit like he smelled to me. He had all those veins in his arms and all and the skin between looked grungy. He looked scaly over all I saw of the guy.

"And bring me a dainty fork," he said. "The daintiest fork you have," he said. "I adore the marrow. Don't you adore the marrow?" he said. "Oh, bingo, bring two forks.

"C'mere a sec," he said.

I leaned closer. The old guy reached up his hand to me and he took a hold of the tie I wore that I—that all of us—have to work in. I put my hands on the table. He was just a light guy. I could feel how light he was. He lifted up out of the chair to me and then he dropped himself back in it again.

"That's better. Oh, that's an improvement," he said.

He took his hat off. He picked a comb out of his pocket.

"Forgive me. I forget," he said.

He pulled the comb through the clump of his hair so his hair curved over the marks on his scalp, a spray of red spots. They looked like BB holes, those spots, in his head. He had put some kind of stuff in his hair, some gel like some of the young guys use that made his head look greasy. His hair was silver.

"That looks good," I said.

I brought him his wine and poured out a glass and pushed the bottle down in a bucket of ice. He pulled out the chair beside him.

"Won't you be so kind?" he asked me.

I checked the clock for Frenchies.

"What the hell," I said. I sat down with the guy.

"Here's to us," he said.

We clinked our glasses. The wine was oaky. Who'd

have thought it could taste so oaky? We polished off
the bottle. It was just me and him by then, and the
Mexican boys in the kitchen. I carried the empty out
into the street and dropped it in the bin outside. I got
the wine list. I thumbed through the whites for the
priciest one and brought it back to the table. I brought
the food out. I brought two forks.

"Hey," I said. I nudged him. "Hey, come on. It's
here."

His hair had slid off to one side of his head and
was spotting the cloth on the table.

"It's suppertime." I nudged him.

"Is this what I asked for?" He sat up. "Are you
certain this is what I asked for?"

He smoothed his hair back, his fingers shining with
the grease he used. The spots I had seen on his head
showed through. They looked hot. They looked hotter,
I thought.

"It's osso buco," I said.

"Ah," he said. "So it is, so it is. Here's to us," he
said. He filled our glasses.

I got a big pile of linen from the hutch and carried
it back to the table; I was worried about the Frenchies.
But I was feeling pretty good by then.

I started folding napkins. I got a little stack of
them going. The guy picked up a napkin from the top
of the stack and shook the creases out of it. He tucked
it into his collar. His hands were shaking. He dabbed
at his neck with the napkin. He dabbed at his mouth.
A little spit bubbled out from between his lips. It was

something. I had to give up on the napkins. He kept picking up napkins from the top of the stack and dabbing at something with them.

"I give up," I said.

The guy sawed at the meat with the knife I brought and got a little chunk cut off. It took him about a month to chew it. You could hear him working the meat around with his tongue, his jaw making big, slow circles. Then he pushed it out into his fingers.

"*Incroyable*," he said.

He placed the meat on the rim of his plate. Selected a leaf of arugula.

I mean, it went on. By the time he had spat out enough of the stuff to garnish the plate with a nasty crown, the Frenchies had started to come.

He put down his knife and his dinner fork.

"I suppose that will do," he said.

He swallowed a little sip of wine. He poked the tines of the tiny fork I had brought into the soft spot of bone and twisted out the marrow. He lowered his mouth to the fork, slipped the marrow off with his tongue.

"Nnnnrrhh," he said. "Gaawww."

It looked like he was trying to swallow. But that he could not.

The Frenchies took seats at the four-top.

The old guy pushed the lump out on his tongue and stroked it off with his finger. He picked up a napkin. He puked a little spot of bile into the bunched-up napkin.

I had started to feel pretty dizzy. One of the Frenchies said my name—something that sounded to me like my name. Maybe it was just some syllable in the language they were talking.

"*Au chocolat,*" said the old guy.

His head had started to wobble. A thread of spit swung down from his mouth. He gaffed me by the neck with his hand. I could smell the food he had chewed up. I smelled the marrow he had scraped out of the boiled shank of bone. I let him kiss me.

"Just a sec," I said.

I got to the walk-in. I got the big bowl down off of the shelf. We keep a spoon in it. But there wasn't a spoon in it. I started scooping the mousse with my hand, dropping it into a soup bowl. I was reeling.

"Here I am!" I called to him from the walk-in. "I'm coming!"

I heard his chair move.

"Stay where you are. It's ready!"

I heard him stumble against the chairs. The Frenchies. The fucking Frenchies. They were shouting.

I put the bowl down. It was cold in there, in the walk-in. Everything was food or metal. Everything, every sound, was muffled. When the old guy stumbled against the chairs, it sounded to me like something big, buried—something bony, moving.

I could taste him. He was on me—the caky way he smelled. I wiped my hands on the floor. I smeared the stuff on the walls in there. The walls were sweating. Everything—all the Cling Wrap was sweating.

Calm down, I told myself.

boulevard

The daughter held the gate open for her to walk through to the field. Against the fence were the horses. Where the horses were inclined to stand, there were bald spots in the field. A fine dust kept falling. At night, the dust disappeared and the bald spots appeared to the daughter like small clouds sunk down. In the dust, the mother's footsteps were as soft as if she had not worn shoes.

It was a night you could smell the river. A hard rain had come from the north and—saffron to the riverbed—enough water for all the fields.

There were laws about the water.

You were only allowed water certain days, certain times.

The daughter brought the chain around to pull fast the gate and the horses shied at the sound this made, and snorted—circling in a slow, breaking canter around the dry field. The fence leaned from the leaning of the horses. Walking the fence line away from her mother, the daughter jostled each post with her hand.

"Candysara," said the mother, "Lady Jane," calling to the horses.

The daughter watched from the mouth of the ditch the horses mill around her mother; only the one mare let her mother come near.

"Candysara," said the mother again.

"Mother?" the daughter had asked. "How do you spell O-h-i—?"

"Why?" the mother had said.

"How do you spell *Ohio?*"

The mother stroked the mare named Candysara in the hollow of her throat and the mare, as though her head were a thing to be carried, gentled her head against the mother's coat. The mother kissed the small white star that marked the face of the mare. In the mother's coat was a deep square pocket the mare had learned to muzzle into. This was why she was called Candysara—the mother's favorite—she came with a whinny to the leaning fence anytime the mother came near the field.

"What are you doing?" the daughter said.

She could hear her mother talking to the horses.

The daughter's horse was Blue One—a white mare, speckled gray, a mare named the name of the color she had turned when rain fell on the field.

The mother walked out from the horses. Past the bald spot where the horses stood, roots clumped where grass had been and the ground was brittle where rain had dried in the deep prints of the horses. Above the ditch that traversed the field, the sound of the leaves of the cottonwoods turning above the daughter was the sound to the mother of water running into the ditch to fill. But the daughter had not remembered: the gates ought not be opened fully, but opened at once. The ditch behind the gate had filled and water so pressed against the gate, the daughter could not raise it. The gate was metal and cool with the coolness of the water that had run down off of the mountainsides into the Rio Grande.

They worked the gate from side to side, their shoes pushing into the slope of silt washed from the river bottom. The metal edge of the gate cut into the bend of their fingers. When water ran out under the gate and tugged at the cuffs of their jeans, the mother said, wanting to rest, "What's this about Ohio?"

The daughter shook her hands out, copying her mother.

"Is there an ocean in Ohio?" the daughter said.

"Why?" said the mother.

"Is there?"

The daughter patted the water with her shoe.

"We've got to get this thing open," said the mother.

She felt the brush of a weed, the small, tapping touch of a stick passing beneath the metal gate in the quickening water. The water's smell, the mother knew from years of snakes in coffee tins—she had let her children keep things—a broken-winged dove the dog brought home, a ringwormed cat. Her own smell, she thought, was of something kept, an old smell, something hoarded.

The daughter had cut the tail of the mare who had blued when rain fell on the field and carried it to her mother, a tail they would pull through a nylon stocking to bend into a drawer to save. In the drawer was the braid of the mother—fine hair banded at either end—a girl's—still flaxen as the daughter's. The daughter's braid had been so long she had threaded the loose ends of it through the back belt loops of her jeans.

Cut short—*pixied,* the mother said—it swung into her face when she bent to the gate again to work it open.

The daughter reached around from behind her mother, saying, "Guess," her fingers cupped over her mother's eyes, saying, "Who is it now, Mother?"

She nickered—a low, caught sound in the daughter's throat, a sound that no longer seemed practiced.

"Lady Jane," the mother guessed.

"Nunh-uh."

"Bubbling Fancy."

"Now?" said the daughter.

She stooped into her mother. They were almost as tall as each other.

"Guess!" the daughter cried. "You're not guessing! Guess again!"

She stamped her foot in the water of the ditch, blotting her lips together.

"B-L-U—"

"I *know*," the mother said.

She had thought as a child they would come to her in the underwater tongue of the leaves—words—how many she could not guess of them nor how they might be said—a spell, a plea, she was certain—you could walk out into them. They would sit like birds on your shoulders; they would light on your hair as they fell.

She heard the slow steps of the horses. The air was cool against her back where the weight of her daughter had been.

"Mother?"

Her mother had said those were mare's tails, but what did that mean? She had said they meant rain coming. When the rain came, the mare had blued, and the sky blued when the sun came up, but those were not the same colors. Those were colors named the same name, but they were different colors. Her name was Melissa—a yellow name, her mother said; she said every name had a color. Different names had the same color and different colors had the same name and mare's tails meant there was rain on the way—high, said her mother, serious clouds that streamed above the mountains. The mountains were named Sandia—"watermelon" in Spanish—because that was the color people thought they turned when the sun went down in the desert. The daughter had not thought you could name a mountain for the soft inside of a fruit, so she had thought of the color of the watermelon's rind, which was the color of the name of her mother.

Was her color like that inside her?

She had not seen where her mother opened.

The sound of the mare, she could make with her tongue, a wet, almost popping sound of pucker and slack, spittle the stallion had tasted. The mare had pushed against the paddock fence and the daughter had leaned back into the fence, helping, holding the mare, saying with the mother, "Whoa, Blue," pushing the fence back into her mother, saying, "That's a girl, now, easy."

It was the skin of the mare that had blued in the rain; her mane and her tail had not. Her tail had lifted over her back and the daughter had seen her winking, the pink clot of flesh as bright as the turned-up lid of an eye. Her father reached under the stallion, helping, guiding him, walking on two legs.

Was that her own smell, a smell not the smell of the mountain color or snakes that swam in the field? Was that the smell of her mother?

"Let me rest a minute," the daughter said.

She could not see the water, but the slow shape of her mother raised up and the water was louder then. She said, more loudly now, "I get so worn down."

"Me*li*ssa," the mother said.

"I do," said the daughter.

The gate trilled against its brace, opened but for the bottom edge the water curved past swiftly. The mother leaned into the rush of water.

"Pumpkin," the mother said, "what about the horsies? If they cut off our water before we're finished, what will the horsies do?"

"I don't want to," said the daughter. "I get so worn down."

She was watching her legs, pulled along, hop and bob in the water.

"I hurt my hands," she said. "See?"

When she let go of the weeds on the bank of the ditch to hold out her hands to her mother, the water pulled her down into the ditch to the waistband of her jeans. She giggled. They leaned together into the current.

. . .

The ditch cut the width of the field and past that was the boulevard and then came mountains. The water ran back to the mountains. Snow fell on the mountains and ran in the spring to the river and the river ran into the sea. In spring, the snow got smaller. Some days you could not notice it, but that did not make it not so. *Unso,* the daughter thought. Some of it stayed on the mountains—patches of white the daughter watched—to speckles, a shine in the eye—then nothing but the blank of stone. It would not happen if you watched it. One morning you would wake and see and it would be unso.

She went out along the ditch ahead of her mother, walking with the water. The water pressed her jeans against her faster than she would go.

Weeds that had come from the riverbed, pulled free in the flash of rain, caught on the mother's legs when she walked; the weeds that grew in the silted ditch broke loose and floated—mustard, the mother knew, and ragweed, goathead and loco. Her coat sleeves pulled long. The mother dipped her arms in the water, netting weeds with her hands—the skin of her hands blued to her. She had found them, waking, beside her, on the sheets in bed.

"Come on," the daughter said. "We've got to get these things open."

There were half a dozen smaller gates to let water

throughout the field. The mouths of the gates were
narrow. In the weeds the horses would not eat were
webs the yellow spiders built. The daughter could
not see them, but she beat them down with her
hand.

Water had broken inside the mare. It was different
water—not like water for the field. The field water
broke on stones as it came down the mountains. You
could not hear a mare's water breaking.

They had brought the mare to foal in a clean stall
in the earth-walled barn—at night and in the rain
also, for the rain, it seemed to the daughter, weakened
the mare's skin.

She had said, "You can see right into her."

The mare's milk veins had swelled blue in the rain
or not, thick as a rope used to hobble. The daughter
slept out in the feed room, so close she could hear the
mare eating—sweet feed and warm bran mash, select
flakes of alfalfa. It would only take keeping near the
mare to know no harm would come.

Yet it had not surprised the daughter—that you
could drown as the foal had drowned inside your own
mother.

Hand and elbow, up to where the muscle hooked
into his shoulder's bone, the father had reached up into
the mare to yank the foal out of the mare pinned against
the paddock fence the daughter pushed back into.

She was the daughter.

The places there were to go were the sounds of their names in her hand.

Ohio.
Armathwaite.
Wetumka.
Canarsie.

The women are still walking.

We expect when they reach the gate at the border of the field, something more will have happened. Something more should have been said.

Armathwaite.
Lady Jane—a gray name.
Canarsie.

Blue One was the name of her and—where the dead mare winched by her pasterns lay—a grassless place the horses, for whatever reason, stood. She was the sound their hooves made striking the dry field. She was the dry field.

"Uh-oh," the mother said.

They walked stoppingly, held against the push of

water. Behind them was the spoor of weeds they had netted with their hands.

"Penny," said the daughter.

"Afraid."

The dark shapes of the horses lunged out in the thudding field.

"Afraid?"

"I don't know," the mother said.

The daughter whinnied.

She cantered to school in the morning, practiced dressage in the courtyard.

Horsie, horsie, horsie.

When the horses ran, in their bellies you heard the break and slosh if you rode them. Her mother said that was not water. But it was a sound like water, a place to have tea parties in, a sound where toads at night froze into the gawk of swimming. You could wrench through water, pinch and suck and poke at it; it would never save in it the place that you had been.

There will be no words, Sister—but shape notes to sing out over our dead, over muddied field and boulevard, shopping malls and hospitals our mothers left for coffins. Oh what snare of scars we claim of our

mothers' bodies, what wounds we have stitched ourselves into. Blame us, we beg, forgive us all thanks
and grateful blessings due.

We are coming, Mother.

We will be there soon.

She will know us by our voices, our wild manes,
by our splitting hooves.

three by t. litz

Pay attention to what you are reading. My name is "Tommy Litz." I was born in Columbus, Oh, 1952. When I was small, I had problems. Frequent temporary loss of certain feelings. My education was not up to par.

I was shining shoes in Columbus, Oh, 1962. I am 2-0-6. I am weak in a particular area. "Tommy." Tommy Litz. Green-brown eyes. Gentle. I was interesting in Mildred until she died. We talked of one thing and another.

1145 Three Degree Drive.

Do not be so nervous. Do not be afraid, "Tommy Litz."

Do you know Mikuni-san's warmhearted character?

This is to greet you with love, wishing you are well of health together with all your family. I would like to know more about you and the weather of your country.

As for now, I was wishing something. I am a quality single. I drive a Dodge PU. Please. (Do not be afraid, ladies. If you are afraid, try thinking: "Tommy, Tommy Litz.") Please remain subdued. If you are a large lady, I ask you to consider what you have just read.

P.S. I cramp James Brown. I am the original James Brown.

Pay attention to what you are reading. Pay attention to what you are reading. What you don't understand, please ask.

From,

Tommy (Litz)

Lovelies,

I got drarwrings, etc.

With God's help, I think to make efforts to go ahead and do not let my family down. I love it so much.

As for now, I am in the agropecuary fair together with a beautiful horse parade going by the street (thanks God).

Do you care much for horse parades?

Guess who had the beautiful baby which is 9 mos.?

(There are many questions I would like to ask of you and they are none of my business, except that I care for you and feel I am one of the last links we have of each other.)

1145 Three Degree Drive.

As for Tommy (doo-wop Brown), English has been mastered.

I am a quality civilian, born 1952. Dodge PU. HELL NO, T. LITZ WON'T GO! (It is regrettable for me to make sure how people are thinking of the situation under the war, actually.)

I greet you, lovely, wishing you are healthy.

P.S. (Tommy Litz)

P.S. (S.) Ladies. Please before you debunk the train, check the seat beside of you for your children and/or personal belongings. (Tommy Litz)

"I shoot all cars, trains, boats." This is what Delroy tells us. "But look, but look, but look." (Delroy)

Unwanting their dog, the Leroys shot it.

Unwanting to live in Columbus, Oh, Mr. Leroy drove his aeroplane into the local river.

Unwanting ———, they ———.

I sincerely hope that I for one do not fall under this ideology. I am 2-0-6.

My future goal is to seek a job in the area of radio announcement (in the Big Apple area). Which means, a great big heartless mass of druggies, murderers, et cetera, as we picture the Big Apple area.

Ladies, ladies, ladies. Could you help TOMMY think of some way to let off some self-esteem? HA. 1145 3 deg. drive. I am weak in some particular areas. (O. H. LITZ) (which used to live in Buga.) Our grandmother is very sick and died there (Buga). We used to love her so much.

Sincerely,
Tommy Litz.
I cramp T. Litz (the original).
Anyway so, Sunshine, (why not) let me feel I know you again?

the change in union city

The girls go on down to Verda's to get the place spruced up. They get the dry goods pulled to the lips of the shelves, the pickle loaf back to the freezer. They box the cards, collapse the table.

Opal starts the streamers.

Ida starts at the back of the store, sweeping around the hornets' nests, the arrowheads, the tools. Ida keeps the dust stirred up.

Lola keeps the ladder still. She blows the mold from the surplus cheese that sits in the heat on the counter. The easy jobs are Lola's.

Verda climbs the ladder to pull the wreaths from the shelves where they sit, collecting. She drops the wreaths at Lola's feet, hauls them out to the parking lot.

Ida sings, *Bingle, bangle, bungle, I'm so happy in the jungle, I refuse to goooo.*

Opal is working on RC's chair. She tapes the crepe to the cushioned arms, to the levers, twists it, walking backward, getting up on things to lift the swags to tape the tails to hornets' nests, to scythes and Visqueened windows.

The girls are drinking Pabst Blue Ribbon.

Verda has dyed her hair. She has sorted the mail that has come to the store in the months since RC left there. Verda holds down the fort, keeps the keys. She hoses down the wreaths in the parking lot, hangs them up over the church pew where the head of the fish used to be. On the porch there, where the fish head hung, the boards are brighter, cleaner above the pew. The store is bleached and leaning. The walnut tree beside the porch, even in the early years, tipped up therusting gasoline pumps, shelled the roof, tweaked the tin.

Ida is sweeping softly, stopping to dance a fox-trot with her frizzy broom. When Ida has danced her last dance over the pile in the front of the store, the girls gather around in their nursey flats to sift through the dust for the dimes they have lost, for the jack they have lost from the deck of cards they have stashed with the gin in the bank box. Verda picks out a scrap of paper from the pile and her eyes cloud with a cruddy joy. She shakes the dust off, the insects, commences, cheered by the leaps and slashes, the slant of her husband's hand.

"Tenpenny. Evap milk. Saltines. Marsh cream. That's got to be RC," Verda says. "They God if it ain't RC," she says, "before he went to Memphis."

BRING A BOILED RAISIN CAKE TO YOUR NEXT FUNERAL: that's what the sign in the window says.

RC himself will say little, according to Verda, little being next to nothing, nothing being next to the little the girls hear when Verda delivers her speech in the store about RC to warn them. They are hopeful. They are widows. They have quit taking wreaths to the graveyard. The rest of town has quit taking them, too, if you go by the books that Verda keeps, if you had gone by the dust on the plastic blooms before she hosed the wreaths down in the parking lot; we have quit eating, too, the rest of town, quit drinking, quit bothering with the mail; we have quit feeding our kids and animals, quit wearing boots or cold creams, boxer shorts, quit playing cards—if you tally the stock that Verda keeps, which stays on the shelves for years.

The girls sit on the pew on the porch of the store and drink their Pabst Blue Ribbon. They talk of what RC used to harp on, of what the girls themselves might guess RC will find it worth his while, when he gets to the store, to harp on. One good guess is the rendering plant. The next good guess is Verda. Their voices rise and shudder, talking about RC. They fuss with the ends of their hair. There is Verda's auburn hair, they say. There are the eighteen-wheelers that come, hauling cattle, hauling chickens, shoats to the reopened rendering plant on the road through Union City. There is the new road to harp on. There is the old aluminum mall RC hates on State Route 3. There is State Route 3. Roads, RC hates, and what runs on roads, Airstreams and pickup trucks, motorcars up from Florida to see the dying leaves. He hates the dying leaves, they say. They are switched by now from Pabst to gin, drinking gin from Dixie cups, getting a little lit by now, waiting for RC.

We all of us sit in the drifting leaves waiting for RC, for the rant that began when the railroad tracks our daddies broke their hands to lay quit ever being run on—the Panama Limited and the Seminole, the City of Miami, the long trains to Chicago up from New Orleans. We are an old town, a railroad town, an asterisk of tracks that run to cities we've not been to, will not go to now. The tracks are all grown over now. Even the Whiskey Dick to Paducah, which we used to ride on a liquor run out of this dry county, quit. There are new roads and refrigerator trucks, faster, better ways to freight bananas.

When we see the girls on the church pew, we sit out, too, on our porches to watch, waiting to see RC's face when he sees the signal we have hung at Finn and Pearl in the months he has been in Memphis. The boy who drives the route from Memphis, who comes when we are ailing, who came for RC at the Feed and Seed, guns through the yellow, changing light, swings the hospital car onto Pearl and speeds home to Verda's— past the cow field, the aluminum mall. The stay-at-home boys are drinking pop in the parking lot of the aluminum mall. One of the boys tips his hat at the car. Another waves. They fold their arms across their chests to keep their cardigans against them.

"It wunt August," one says. "Must of been July. It was when I fried that chicken."

"No, Vern," another says. "We was in the shade. Every living soul with a lick of sense, we was all of us in the shade. We was drinking something."

"Sure, Arnold, drinking. We was in the shade."

"If you got the sense God gave a goose, why, you was in the shade, okay?"

"Okay, Arnold."

"Hot, oh, August," Arnold says. "Why, it was a hunnerd degrees. We was drinking something."

"Drinking, yeah. You said that."

"Lemonade!" Arnold says, remembering. He twists the ring on his finger. "Here he is in his boots coming down from the store and it a hunnerd degrees!"

"Arnold?" Vern says.

"Yeah?" says Arnold.

"Better hush, Arnold. Sit down. Better let me tell it."

RC, he never sees the boys, going through town that last time. He never sees the four-way light.

The car swoops down over the river, flashes up the steep hill the livestock trucks grind up and then skids off, a popping turn in the gravel lot that makes RC—suppose it makes him feel queasy. He sees the silver heads of the girls, the auburn, recalls talcumy smells and glycerin soap, the terror of purses and shoes. RC lowers his head to his knees as the girls negotiate the steps of the porch, steady themselves on the gasoline pumps as they cross the lot to the car.

"Mr. Brooks," says the boy from Memphis, "sit up now. This is your wife and friends."

RC crouches until he hears them shuffling beside the doors of the car and then he sits up, cocks his head in the window. Sees nothing but the slumpy loveliness of females drinking gin. Ida lets herself drop to one knee on the concrete slab where the gas pumps sit and spoils the moment for him; she starts to cry—dry, choking sounds—and soon everyone is at it; even his Verda is at it, who hasn't cried since her own wedding night in 1923. RC keeps moving his head around to cast his one eye over them all, except for Opal; he tries not to look at Opal, as big as she is, and talky.

"Well, me," Opal is saying. "Will you lookit that? Will you lookit that?"

RC looks like something gone soft in the ground all the hard winter long, his body boneless, his face bunched off to one side. The skin of his face is slick as clay and crawling, spattered with yellow scars.

Opal dabs at her nose with a tissue, reaches for Verda's hand.

"I tried to tell you," Verda says. "I told you."

She tries to think what her husband looked like when he looked like himself at all. RC's heart knocks. His mouth gets parched.

"Y'all don't stroke out," Lola says to them all. "Everbody breathe."

They do, a shallow, helpless wheezing.

The boy comes around and opens the door and swings RC's thick legs out. "I got to go, ma'am. Let's move," he says.

Verda tips in, kisses RC on the side of his head that has got his face still on it. She works an arm underneath her husband's legs, slings her other arm behind his back, says, "Come on, Pop. Let's get you in. We have fixed your store so pretty."

Before his dog died, before the TV, and the do-less days that did him in, the days that we quit coming, RC swept and stocked the store, provided, profited, tallied the bills in the bank box—before the gin and cards, before the bulk of RC's bitch went off on the grill of a livestock truck on the road through Union City. Which is why, we say, he got the TV, tallying, too, the new road, the four-way light, the litter, tallying the loggers, their rotgut, hard-mouthed wives. Floridians, we tally, sausages in cans, motorcars and moon walks, the chalky bed that used to be the river RC fished from.

RC, he pulled his boots off. That's what we say in town.

He took to letting Ida slub his feet while, on the TV, brassy, hulking lunks beat their chests in the golden light—Valiant Val Sandini, the Invincible Flavius Ray—squawkers, strutters, rubbering off the ring ropes through the dogless autumn, the seasons of deer and squirrel.

The walnuts drop and dimple the roof and roll off onto the gravel lot. When it was RC's daddy's store and we skidded our bikes on the broken shells, we knew from the far-off shrill of the train how hard we had to ride to reach the tracks before it passed on—past the icehouse and the Leader store, before the new Winn-Dixie, before any of this that will come to pass had made its way to town.

The days go along like this now: RC in his barber chair, eating graveyard stew. The Knights of Columbus go see him. Kiwanis goes with chicken salad, the sixth-grade class with bright balloons they have painted rainbows on. Motorists from Florida slow and stop and soft-shoe in, blinking from the sun.

"Leaf peepers!"

"Junior Leaguers!"

"Philanthropists!"

"Baptists!"

Opal could cut out their tongues.

It is not that she hates a long-tongue, who loved, after all, RC. Hadn't all the girls loved RC, after all? A wide man, a talker. *A story! A story! Tell us about Sarasota, RC. Sweet thing. Love.*

But he won't speak; RC won't eat—but to eat bread soaked in sweetened milk, Verda's graveyard stew.

But to eat, the first sound RC makes, he makes when his buddy Buddy comes to tell a little RC story.

"RC, he's down to the corner, like that, standing at Finn and Pearl. He's walking up and down the sidewalk. He has got his binocs on. I say, 'What're you doing out here, RC?' "

Buddy keeps his coat on, leans against the counter in the draft of the open door. "Don't you know he is out there trying to keep the *elephants* out of town."

"Elephants?" Opal says. "That's ridiculous. Ain't no elephants around here."

This makes RC snort; he brays, and the milky phlegm from the graveyard stew spits through his pinched-up nose.

"God above," says Opal.

She gets behind him, hooks her arm around his neck to keep him in his chair.

"Oh, pitiful, pitiful man," Lola says. "I have got to go home."

Lola is the first to quit them.

Ida goes to the bank box, fills her Dixie cup with gin. She says, "Can't a fellow laugh ever once in a while?"

"Why, Ida," Verda says.

"Well, can't he?"

"Yeah, ma'am," Buddy says, "that's what *I* say," moving to the door. " 'RC,' I say, 'when's the last time you seen a elephant around here?' He kindly gets his eye up so. He's shaking his change in his trousers. 'I's doing a pretty good job, ain't I? Pretty darn good job,' he says."

Buddy never comes back. Lola stays away.

Verda keeps the high shelves stocked. Every can of peas the girls eat from the shelves, Verda replaces with two cans, pulling the old cans forward, sliding the new behind. Nothing leaves the shelves but what the girls eat, and they feel they have eaten nothing.

The days grow colder. Opal goes out with the wheelbarrow, foraging for wood. Ida feeds a slow fire in the woodstove. They make suggestions—cold-weather soups and pot roast, greens with ham and bacon grease, the way he likes greens, the way they

know that RC likes greens. But all he will eat is
graveyard stew.

After school, the kids come with their lunch pails,
open the pails at RC's feet to pick out what they have
saved him—bologna scraps and ribbon snakes and
lumps of macaroon. The schoolgirls try to feed him.
The boys pocket gum and candy; they scorch snakes
and toads on the top of the stove.

"What happened to you, RC?" the boys ask.

"What happened to RC?" ask the girls.

Here is how Verda tells it: RC, he had a accident.
We sit; we wait. Weeks pass, years.

RC, he had a accident.

RC, he had a accident. Shot hisself in the head.

"Remember that old Ford, RC? The one my
momma drove? We would drive it down here for a
fill-up—it was about the only place I think Momma
ever drove. It was still your daddy's place. The gasoline
pumps wasn't busted up like they are right now.
RC"—Verda breathes in and looks at him—"things
should have been took care of."

RC sits there with his head full of shot, looking
like he is listening, and then like he is not. He starts
twitching in his barber chair, working it up to pitch
and squeak, trying to keep enough noise in the store
that he can't hear Verda talk.

She says, "Momma'd go in and buy some things while I sat in the sun in the car. I watched the mirror to see you coming. I don't guess I recall ever coming to the store without you letting the door slam to and walking across the lot out there to lean on the car and talk. My God, RC. You'd lay your arms on the car like you do and talk about, I don't know, fishing. It didn't matter. I never did care what you talked about. I just liked to see you."

RC is quiet again, listening. The other girls are listening. Verda smoothes back her hair and goes on.

"Momma'd come back out and get in the car and say good-bye to you. Then she'd start to pull the car out. But you would never move, RC. You never would quit talking. You'd be leaning on the car while it moved off with your arms rubbing over the rooftop, still looking like we were there. I'd watch in the mirror to see you. I was too shy to turn around. Pretty soon I didn't want to see you at all in the mirror or any other way, except I couldn't help it. I'd tell Momma to hurry up—because I heard you still, and I thought to myself, When he stops talking—I remember telling Momma this—saying, 'Momma, if he stops talking, he will fall like a tree in the dust.' We would just, Momma and I—what could we do?—keep driving."

It is not in the blood of any of us to know quite how to tell it, to tell quite what we know.

We are liable to start in the thick of it, with the

hot spell, say, the heat of the day RC came to town and shot up the signs where the signal hangs, before the signal hung there, before he went off to the aluminum mall and shot up the back of the aluminum mall, or after, no, before then. Arnold, Vern, making their way up to Verda's store with the rest of the boys behind them, try, as they go, to tell it, to figure what all it was RC sprayed with shot the August day the car took him off to Memphis—stop signs, sure, the aluminum mall, the ass end of a livestock truck—bickering, the stay-at-home boys, bogging down on the order of things, the sequence of the day's events, the details, the lemonade, the heavy boots he wore.

All of what RC filled with shot before he got behind the Feed and Seed, you can get, in time, from Arnold. That the livestock truck RC shot up was soughing in the parking lot while the driver lagged with Verda, let his tongue grow long with Verda, drinking sour beer—for all of that, ask Arnold.

You can get none of it from Verda. From Verda, you will get that he bungled his soul, by accident, with buckshot—nothing about the six-legged dog, nothing about the livestock truck.

Should Arnold omit the early hours, which he is almost sure to do, the cooler dark before the spree that set the day in motion—ask Ida, who will tell you about the head of the fish that hung on the wall on the front of the store for years until it was stolen, sneaked off early that August day that looked like any other day except we saw them—Arnold first in his silly hat, dragging the fish through town, and after, in the heat souping off the blacktop, RC marching down in his heavy boots, an armed and only posse come to take back what was his. It was high drama for this bottomed-out town we none of us saw to the end of. We were porch-sitting, spectating, leaving it to run its course with the stupid, stunted eyesight of people accustomed to nothing happening.

Ida says, "Remember that old beagle, RC? Remember that fellow Flavius Ray we used to see on TV?"

The balloons deflate; the streamers fray. The feathery cloak of mold grows back on the surplus cheese.

Ida sings a bit of something. "Remember that, RC?"

All the answer RC makes is to snort and bray when she hangs her head and paces in front of the woodstove. *Giraffe,* Ida says, and *kangaroo, hippopotami,* and *elephant.*

"When's the last time you saw a kangaroo come through Union City?" she says.

She polishes off the gin.

"Ah hah!" Ida says.

RC wags his finger, raises what is left of his eyebrow on the side that is left of his face.

"Say it one more time, Ida, and I will knock you upside down," Opal says, and she would; Opal says she means it—but RC is laughing so hard by now, he is all anyone can hear.

The schoolgirls quit coming to feed RC. The boys come back with their lunch pails until they have stolen everything in Verda's store fit for boys their size to steal, and then go elsewhere after school.

The girls try to make an afghan, each taking her turn with the crochet hooks in the easy chair by the stove. Opal, her big hands stiff, quits before even a corner is hooked. Ida lets the ball of yarn catch fire underneath the woodstove, sinks deeper into the easy chair through the mildewy hue of the days. The days, the girls know, keep passing. They know the ground might freeze—despite the heat and fire glow, despite the way the same dream repeats itself inside.

They try to keep things spruced up. The streamers Opal strung from RC's chair wilt and tear and Verda tapes the torn ends back together. She unties the balloons; Opal plumps them up; Ida ties them back again. They are tacking balloons to the rafters when the stay-at-home boys show up at the store with a dew of sweat settled onto their lips, with their buttons pulled to popping, flushed to talk about RC.

"Heavens, yes," the girls say. "Goodness, yes. Yes, yes, you boys come ahead on in."

And they do. And they all, even the dandiest, get to drinking Pabst from cans.

Arnold gets to talking about his truancy from school, about a switching he took for a school day skipped some sixty years ago when the carnival came to town.

"Naw, Arnold," says another old boy, and Arnold says, "Say?"

"Nineteen ten, you tell me?" says the other. "You saying 1910 it came?"

"Did I say 1910?" Arnold says. "Because would I say 1910," he says, "if it wasn't for 1910 it came? It was 1910, I tell you."

"Naw, Arnold. That ain't it."

"It's it," says Arnold.

"It ain't," says the other.

And so on, and so on, until Opal says, "Shit, boy," and walks off to the back of the store to fetch more cans of beer.

Verda pops the tops off, passes the cans around. She presses her beer against RC's neck so he knows how cold they feel.

"Okay, so 1910," Ida says. "You was, oh, eleven."

It is not until much later—not until after they have brought RC on the bed of Arnold's truck through town—that the girls know it is Arnold who stole the fish, the proof of RC's fish story, and remember then these waiting days when they sat with Arnold at RC's feet and shared their Pabst Blue Ribbon.

"I took a licking with a hickory switch to see that goddamn cow," Arnold says. "And do you know," Arnold says, turning now to speak to RC with a sudden, beery boldness, "you, RC, you said that cow, you said that cow had two heads." RC's eye blinks open and Arnold stops hearing himself at all. "Two heads! Two heads!" he shouts, getting louder, looking up at RC, seeing the murky calm of the eye left to RC to open. *"Lookee, boys!"* Arnold barks, a good carny shrill. *"You flash 'em, we'll cash 'em. Never in the history of the world!"*

Arnold tries to stand, drops back, falls with his hands in his pockets.

Ida pats him on the knee.

"It was nothing but a hump of bone," Vern says, seeing that Arnold is quiet, "why, a funny lump of muscle."

Ida takes her hand from the old man's knee and, kneeling on the floor behind him, rubs his chest with her fingertips, saying, "Arnold, Arnold," searching, finding with her hand the tiny hurt lodged in his heart these years.

Here they are on the church pew with a quilt drawn across their legs: Opal, Arnold, Ida, lined up big to small. The wreaths hang above their heads.

The rest of the boys are home asleep, worn out with the thrill of the two-headed cow, the six-legged pup, the Negress—the early signs, they claim, of the hopeless sump of RC's later years.

Verda is in the store with a bucket, sponging RC down.

"Maybe you boys are right," Opal says.

"Say?" Arnold says.

"Maybe that's where this started."

Opal waits for the old man to say something. "With RC, I mean. I'm saying if it's true," Opal says, "because it might be."

"What do you mean?" says Arnold.

"I'm only just saying what you said. You're the one what said it."

"He was rolling in the hay with that Negress!" Arnold says. "That's what I said!"

"Will you stop it?" Ida says. "You two, you, Opal, please."

Ida turns the quilt back, and she walks back behind the store and cries in the high weeds.

She thinks of polio and yellow fever, whiskey wars, locusts, barn-burning and church-burning and the floods of '42. The Mississippi frozen as far south as Vicksburg, girls.

The things RC has told them!

But the Negress is something new.

Ida walks farther out away from the store, stumbling over the harrowed ground that used to be RC's garden. The ground is soft still, weedy, softest under Ida's feet in the weedless place she had helped RC dig the hole for the six-legged dog. Ida sees RC's pale body, cloudy in the Visqueen tacked to the windows at the back of the store. She thinks of the six-legged dog, the generations of six-legged beagles, the best bitch saved from every litter, the one whose legs were long. She thinks of what care RC took with what there was to be found of the dog, how he arranged it in the trough of clay, placed it back together. When he had gotten the dog arranged, Ida helped him gather the bright broad leaves of the cucumber magnolias that grew where the river used to flow, helped him lay them along in a bright, green sheet above the bloody pieces.

Ida sees Verda moving around her husband, sponging him down, drying him. Her knees give in a little. She sees him lift his arms up—as if to hang from something, as if he is waiting, Ida thinks, as the Negress must have waited to fly from her trapeze.

RC drops his arms and Verda makes him lift them up again. She must have known about the Negress. She doesn't think about the Negress. She tries to think instead how RC looked in the days he used to come and hang his arms on her mother's car. It becomes almost all she can think of, the way he might have been.

She scrubs his chest, his belly. She has to steady his flesh with her hand, pull the folds of his skin smooth to clean him. She finds grayish strips at the bottoms of the folds she scrubs with her sponge to slough up. She finds ribby spots on his member, whitish patches where the skin was cut to graft to the skin of his head.

All of this, we could leave out. We know RC would. Seeing Ida back behind the store where the garden used to be, Verda, we know, would forget the day the dog got hit by the livestock truck, forget the whole season—the early peas and the Silver Queen in the garden coming on.

The next day, the dog dead, the first day and the last RC ever darkened any door of the aluminum mall, he bought himself a TV. He left the P.O. and the bank box keys and caught the bus to Paducah to buy a case of gin.

Ask anyone. Ask Ida. Ida will tell you he called his wife to stay awhile while he dug the grave and watch him, talk to him—and that Verda never came, she will say. RC gathered what was left of his dog, on the blacktop, in the weedy ditch, in the broken glass and beaten shoes, the soot of the sloping shoulder. He found shreds of ear and paw pad, patches of yellowish belly skin, carried them back to the place he would dig in the new green shoots of corn.

Verda, please, come on here, talk to me while I dig.

She dusts his crotch with talcum. She pulls his pants on. She pulls a fresh shirt down over his head and walks him back to his barber chair, moving slowly, letting the hour resume its groove, its old trick of nothing changing that makes a life hold still.

The next time the boys come back, Ida hears that the Negress never flew from a trapeze. The Negress, according to Arnold, was a dwarf who twirled from a length of rope looped through a hoop in her nose. The girls watch RC to see in him a hint of some objection.

"Swear to God," Arnold says. "What she hung on by her nose."

RC gapes and twitches.

"That's enough," Verda says. "He's hungry."

"He's not hungry," Ida says. "He's thinking about that Negress."

She makes a hoopy shape with her fingers, spins, her head thrown back, the tips of her thumb and finger hooked into her nose.

"That's right, that's right," Arnold says, clapping. He doesn't know whether the twirling dwarf was something he saw or heard of.

Verda climbs in RC's barber chair, lifting out the hem of her dress so she can straddle his knees and feed him. "Mercy," she says, "Ida, the way you carry on."

When RC gapes, she slips the spoon between his bunched-up molars.

They hear, the boys, RC feeding, the clatter of RC's tongue. They hear the suck and creak in his throat when RC tries to swallow.

RC, he had a accident.

RC, he had an old dog; he had a two-headed cow.

He carnied from town to town, to towns as far off as Sarasota. It's no accident, the boys think, the shape RC is in now. Think back to 1910, they think, trying not to hear in the sounds he makes anything familiar, anything quite like the sounds they hear in the rooms where they live alone. If you had known RC back then, they say. Back then, they say—in what RC calls his glory years, the dirty-shirt days of the carnival—that's where the seed of what would happen is, of what has happened now. It's no accident, no wonder now, that they themselves are shining—church-going, stay-at-home boys who dandy through these afternoons since RC came from Memphis, oh, their bowlers brushed, their good shoes buffed, their wives dead and their wedding rings dropped in their trouser pockets.

RC kicks his chair, pointing. Verda twists open a fresh loaf of bread to make more graveyard stew. Ida makes herself dizzy spinning with her fingers hooked in her nose.

They stand in front of him, trying to see what RC sees; his eye, they see, isn't looking at all at what he looks to be pointing to. He is pointing at her, Opal thinks. Ida, moving to him, thinks he is pointing at her. She pulls a stool up, slubs the skin from his ankles, filthy, flicks it—like she used to do when she sat with RC on the church pew, watching TV.

"Remember in the afternoon them wrestlers came onto the TV?" Ida says. "Fancy, my, brocade, their backs all greased and bright."

"Oh, Ida," Verda says.

"Well, they did," Ida says. "Remember? Tell her the truth, RC."

It could be the smell of something. It could be the way Ida looked as she turned, softening, dizzy, giving in to the pull of her own hand, her fingers hooked in her nose. RC cannot say but to say he remembers, seeing Ida, not the Negress he loved from the carnival, but the fish he hauled up onto the beach—the grand finale, the gaping, scaly trophy that cinched his glory years.

"You got any cards?" Arnold says.

"Cards?" Verda says.

"I thought I read it in the paper you won a tournament somewhere. But I ain't seen you playing."

"I been busy," Verda says.

"Oh, I know. He takes tending. You got to watch him all the time. Hey, Ida, honey, you play bridge? Because maybe you could teach me. I don't believe Verda will teach me," Arnold says. "She's got too much on her mind."

"I'll teach you," Verda says.

"You're tired," Arnold says. "You got RC to fuss with."

"I ain't tired," Verda says.

"Besides which," Arnold says, "I could never learn."

He picks at a thread on his trousers. "You really think I could learn it, Verda?"

"I said so."

"I read the book, okay, I studied," he says. "Royal flush and whatnot. But it's hard, it's hard. 'Course, I ain't actually played the game. Now I got time to play it, of course, my Eloise is dead."

Verda finds the cards in the bank box, sets up the

flimsy table. Arnold makes a face to indicate he is thinking about it still. Then he shuffles up, sits down, hops his chair up close to the table.

It is a trick to see.

RC, since he lost his one eye, has had to see with his other eye; he has had to hear with the one ear that is mostly still where it ought to be. He sees Arnold, or not, Buddy, or Vern, bellying up to the table. He sees Verda's hair go from auburn to something like tangerine. For months now, winter now turning into spring, the store has gotten smaller, quiet to him and gray. He hears the woodstove cooling through the afternoon. His wife is in the kitchen. His wife is playing cards. Unless he sees them side by side, the girls look all the same to him. None of them ever look to him to be any nearer than all the others, any farther than everything else in the store he can focus his eye to see.

RC sees himself for the first time in the curving lens of the camera Arnold brings to the store. He kicks his chair, pointing.

"What in the world?" Verda says. She arranges herself behind RC, with her hair done up like a question mark. She is wearing her emerald earrings that touch her neck when she moves.

"Keep still," she says. "Smile, RC."

He keeps pointing to the door.

"You hungry?" Ida says.

"Ready?" Arnold says, and Verda smiles.

"You want a foot rub?" Ida says. "You want to watch TV?"

RC nods his head wildly.

"We're trying to take a picture, Ida. Why don't you go outside?" Arnold says. He snaps a picture. He will bring it back on porcelain and stash it in the bank box.

"Go outside?" Ida says.

A cry breaks from RC's throat that sounds more dog than human. "He wants to go outside!" Ida says. "Lookit here, I got it!"

The four of them—Opal and Ida on one side, Verda and Arnold on the other—make a throne with their arms to bear him out, to sit him down on the church pew. RC twists in the pew and swipes at the wreaths Verda has hung on the wall. He knocks a bloom off. He knocks a wreath off its nail in a puff of dust and it drops behind the church pew.

His eyelid flutters. He sucks his cheeks between his teeth, winks his lips together. His lips start turning blue.

"God above," says Opal.

He sucks his cheeks in deeper and, with his finger, flattens the fleshy tip of his nose so that it looks to be even less a nose than a pair of holes in his head. The girls try not to look at him, at the new mess he is making, piggish, fishy, of the face they have come to know.

"Quit," Verda says. "That's enough, RC."

She shakes him by his shoulders, but he won't quit. She shakes him harder, his neck limp, his head making a funny, rubbery sound when it knocks against the wall. RC tries to think back. He knows the fish head hung there, above the pew where the wreaths are now. But he cannot remember it quite, how it looked there, forgot, before they carried him out, that it would not be there at all. He does not mind, he is grateful, even, for the sound of his head when it knocks against the wall. It keeps him thinking.

RC thinks of the crappies he used to catch when the river used to flow. He hears in the sound of his own head the sound the heads of the crappies made when he hit them against a stone. He didn't mind that. But it took a whole string of them—slender, fine-boned things—to dent a big man's craving, to feed the growing hunger RC felt back then. Crappies, hell, RC thinks, who would sooner be a giant eased out of the Gulf of Mexico, an eyesore, a hazard, flesh enough to feed for days a town like Union City, bones as thick as fingers, talk, sooner, RC would be, a lasting trouble, a mighty rottenness that never goes away.

They settle in beside him. Arnold pulls the strip from the Polaroid and they huddle in to watch it make, to see it changing. Verda thinks she sees in it something of the boy she knew. This sends her to the bank box to pat around in the webby dark, feeling for the flaking envelope, the rotten elastic band.

"Here you are with that cow," Verda says. "Here is that old beagle."

She passes RC the photographs he remembers from the carnival, and he remembers that this is the way he has seen since the day he came from Memphis, the day the days started turning, even before they passed, into a glossy flatness, a shabby souvenir.

Ida scoots up against him, leaning in to see. She is perfumed, Ida, these springy days; her earlobe, poked through her netted hair, brushes RC's chin. She listens to him breathing.

A slow leak of blood from his scalp—the skin split when he struck his head—dribbles around from behind his neck.

"Ida, move. Let me in there." Verda dabs at his neck with a tissue. "Let me please sit down."

Ida, giving up her seat, takes the envelope from Verda, slips the photos from RC's hand. She paces in front of the church pew, holding her hands behind her. She walks the way that RC walked, the floorboards squalling.

"Back in the hungry, runaway years when you were ten, eleven," Ida says—she has his preachy way of speaking—"you went off with the carnival, walked off in your boots down the dirt road that ran through the harrowed bottomland, leading your six-legged beagle, leading your borrowed cow."

The cow had a freaky canker, a mushy malignancy growing up from its shoulder bone. It is what made the cow a two-headed cow, a sidebar for the knee-high horse, a two-for-one enticement that fished the nickels from schoolboys' pockets.

"You got as far off as Sarasota," Ida says, "isn't that right, RC?"

She walks the photographs of Sarasota along, pausing a time with each of them in front of each of their faces—blue days, pictures of blue days, of sequined girls in ostrich plumes, barefoot in a froth of tide, clapping at RC.

Here is RC on a cinder block, trying to hold his fish up; he has slipped his arms under the giant gills and hefted the fish as high as his chin, as high as it looks like he is able, without being nearly able to lift its tail out of the sand.

Its tail, we remember, was silver. We remember a cart on the courthouse steps, a scrap-wood contraption with a worn tarp tossed across it. We remember the brittle horn RC blew until the houses emptied, the photographs, wicking sweat, he pulled from his back pockets.

"What in the world?" we asked him. He was pacing on the courthouse steps—a boy still in his limber years, his leg swelled stiff to a man's size from drinking bad shine.

"You had to swing the damn thing around you," Ida says, "plant it out in front of you, vault from your hip to walk then."

RC stuck his horn in the top of his boot and told of floods and devil winds, of gypsies who shat dia-

monds, of harp-in-the-pulpit preachers barking charms
to lure the snakes in. We passed around the photographs, mouthing our suspicions. He spoke of nights
of pounding rain, the hardships of bitter cold, the road
home from Paducah. He got to the part where he had
hooked the fish with a chicken leg in the whitecapped
surf and the sheriff came forward with his brindle dogs
to scrutinize the scrap-wood cart. He lifted the tarp
by a grommet, bowing to look in.

We remember!

We remember how the hair pricked up, a spiky
ridge up the spines of the dogs who sniffed at the cart
and then lunged at it. RC swung his jake leg at them.
The sheriff, who had the leashes of his brindle dogs
looped around his knuckles, toppled and came with
the head of the fish slopping down the stairs.

It was a fish we had not seen the likes of.

It had gilded scales, tiny teeth!

It had a giant sticky eye as big as the plates we
ate from.

The scales were strewn on the courthouse steps,
and shy at first, we fell in, seeing Arnold Crabtree
crushing fistfuls into his pockets. He was pinching his
nose, taunting RC.

He taunts him now, an unbeliever, an old man
sitting on a church pew. Arnold does not give in to
the story, or seem to the girls to, to the old thrill of
it. But we ourselves know better. We have seen what
the girls have not: Arnold, collapsed on the road, trying

to drag the fish head home; we have dropped, ourselves, to our hands and knees and looked through the low, cloudy pane and seen it in his cellar.

Arnold fingers the photograph, guesses again at the sleight of hand that could dwarf such a lanky, jake-legged boy as RC in those days had been: RC holding the fish by its crimson gills—straining, smiling, standing on a cinder block with the tail of the fish still dragging.

"Be ashamed," Ida says, "you ought to," and snatches the photograph from him.

Opal reminds Arnold that the fish was so big, RC had to build a scrap-wood cart to haul its head back home in. She says, "Remember, Arnold, the tracks you saw on the old road from Paducah?"—the last place the carnival took RC, the Paducah road dust and washboard then that the stay-at-home boys refused to believe RC had walked the whole of, though he had, Opal says. "Remember?"

He took the boys out to show that he had, saying, *See? This here is the track the cart wheels make. This is my mark my boot makes that I drag on the goddamn ground.* RC pointed out to the stay-at-home boys the leatherless toe of his steel-toed boot, the roadside stretch of parentheses his bad-leg boot had left in the dirt—the jake leg the leg that would leave the mark of a thing that had ended, the finishing parenthesis of RC's ruinous years.

. . .

Arnold comes first thing the next morning. He has been thinking about Paducah, he says.

Verda feeds RC his breakfast.

Arnold picks at the surplus cheese.

"Wouldn't it be nice?" he says.

"What's that?"

"Paducah."

He walks to the chair with a crumb of cheese and holds it out to RC. He says, "Come on, Verda."

When Ida comes, she calls Opal, and Opal arrives in her yellow dress. Verda wears gloves and a pillbox hat and sits in the truck with her hands in her lap while Arnold and Opal get in on either side of her. Arnold arranges his arm against Verda's neck, along the back of the seat of the truck. They wave good-bye to Ida.

The concrete road to Paducah, Ida knows, is newly blacktopped, the days it used to take to go becoming shorter hours, the road beneath become so smooth, a body barely knows that she has gone when she has come back. When the sound of the truck has died away over the hill from Verda's store, Ida cuts away the Visqueen, opens a high window. She pulls away the streamers, the tattered crepe springing free and slowly twisting down. She piles the crepe with the slack balloons she snaps away from the rafters, carries the pile behind the store and drops it in the weeds.

RC is sleeping easy. She slips his socks off. She fills a bucket.

The trouble was, the first time, the shotgun, the

buckshot, and RC alone at the Feed and Seed, delirious and weary. Ida knows enough to use a bullet to get it done right this time.

She finds a sponge, a bar of soap. RC moves his head around, waking up, looking out for Verda. Ida tugs his shirt off, lathers his chest and arms. She lets him work his finger in under the band of her girdle.

When she has gotten RC cleaned up, and gotten the gun cleaned and loaded, Ida fills two cups with gin. She finds the photograph, the one that Arnold took, in the bank box, and she slips it into her girdle until she is ready to show it to RC. They drink the gin; she cracks his toes, clips his curling toenails.

In the photograph, Verda's hair is brilliant. Her face looks smooth and young. RC's one eye has wandered. The shadows cast by the overhead light collect in the hole in RC's face where his other eye used to be.

Ida strokes his eyelid, touches her lips to his thumb.

"It's all right," she says. "This old life, RC. This old scrubby nothing."

When the others get back from Paducah, Ida tells them, "RC, he did it again. He did it again. Go see."

We turn out.

We close the stores and the schools to see them drive RC's pine casket on the bed of the truck through town. Never mind the aluminum mall; never mind the stop signs. We elbow, we bustle and weep on the sidewalks to toss our coins and flowers in when Arnold's truck creeps by.

When the truck swings wide to take the turn, we retrieve our shovels. We do not carry them out to Laurel Dale where the rest of the husbands are buried. We go back among the Silver Queen that volunteers each spring.

We rest, and dig, and rest a time. We get our ropes rolled under the casket.

There are wreaths, of course, shoots of corn; there are the pearly, wafery scales we are saving in our pockets.

We toss the coins onto the burnished clay, the flowers. The clay sticks to the blades of our shovels.

Here is how we tell it: RC, he had a accident.

We cannot remember all of it. We cannot begin to tell it quite the way RC would have told it.

We sit; we wait.

Arnold is hauling the head of the fish up the hill in a wagon, its wide mouth tattered, its eye a mucky blue.

"That's good," Verda says. "That's good, old man. This way, we can bury it with him."

We leave a portrait on the headstones of the dead of Union City. There are portraits of Ida and her husband, of Opal and hers, on the faces of the granite in

Laurel Dale that mark where their husbands lie. They are imposed on porcelain ovals: Ida in a blue dress, Opal in yellow. Below them, past the hyphen that follows the day they were born, is a flat stretch with a modern gloss to be chinked on the day they are buried.

It is our way of letting the men of our town take their wives to the grave.

If you come to our town, take State Route 3 up the hill to the store. You will see where the storefront is brighter—the clean shade beneath the plank where the head of the fish was hung.

We have been sitting along the porch steps, sitting along the church pew. See where our pants and skirts have smudged the skiff of pollen?

It is how you will know we have been here. It is how you will know we have gone.

amharic

Injera is bread.

Wiha is the word for water.

Tejj is a wine made from honey, drunk thick from a slim-mouthed vase.

We were two.

"In our country . . ." he began.

I did not drink the water. The *tejj* was poured from a blue teapot carried low against a big man's leg. It was a tin room, without windows. Two boys kicked a ball beyond the door. A ball is a wad of plastic wrapped with what string there is.

He tore away a piece of *injera*.

We had each washed one hand.

Injera is softer than other bread, cool and damp, like the touch of certain fingers. There are pores. It is as large as the platter it is served on, or larger, the fringe of it overhung. But I was not hungry.

"Eight years of water and *injera*," he said. "For eight years, home was a cell so small, I could not turn around. The ceiling touched my head."

There were new moons of dirt beneath the fingernails of his just-washed hand.

It was a time of many days, many places.

Beyond the door, a third boy came, smaller than the others, his small legs bowed; also a goat, dragging its tether.

"In the time of the revolution," the man said, "children were picked up off of the streets by soldiers. The soldiers asked them where they lived."

Yedoro wot is a preparation of highly spiced fowl, mostly chicken, ladled onto *injera* beside a mound of ground beans. To eat, you tear away a piece of *injera*, beginning with the fringe, working inward. Into this, cupping *injera* in your hand, you pinch *yedoro wot*, beans. The hand works like a claw.

"They would carry the children to their homes," the man said, "to their parents. Do not imagine that the soldiers would not wait if the parents happened not to be home. That the parents watched, that they were made to watch, this was part of it."

Tena yisTillin is "hello."

The hand works like a claw.

Addis Ababa means "the new flower," a name chosen by the Empress Taitu, who was barren, and who was buried in a hill above the hills of the city. In Addis Ababa, when a child is born, the afterbirth is buried on either side of the door to the house. For a male child, it is buried to the right of the door in hopes he will find his way. The afterbirth of the birth of a girl goes to the left of the door to the house, in the path of the man she will marry.

I cannot say what difference there is between losing your right or your left hand, having lost neither hand, and having known only, in the path of my life, the private revolutions of the privileged. The hand had been lopped off, well above what would have been the man's wrist, and not long before the time I speak of. These are mere assumptions, of course, based on how I see.

He chewed loudly, his mouth open.

Skin had puckered over the blunted limb as though the hand were not lost but had in some way retreated, pulled back, fisting skin into the flesh of the man's arm, the arm bloating, yellow as old bruise.

Carrying me, my mother dreamed my body moved through her, into her neck, her shoulder. I moved into the back of her hand.

The blunt end of the man's arm clenched and bloomed. It lay beside the food, on the burlap top of the table.

Amesegginallehu is "to give thanks."

Peristalsis is what makes your food go down.

Esophagitis had seized the throat of my father.

"In our country," the man said, "we feed the old and the very young and those who travel from other places. *Gusha* is like a kiss," he said, "a gesture of thanks, or welcome."

The man lifted the food to me, a handful of fowl and beans wrapped in damp bread.

It was a time also of dreams. In one dream, I live with my family in a farmhouse in middle Ohio.

I used to feed my father. I used to stroke the skin of his throat, not altogether gently, trying to make the food go down. He was not an old man then.

He leaned toward me. The tips of his fingers touched my teeth, the inside skin of my lips. His name? I cannot pronounce the man's name, though if it mattered, perhaps I could spell it.

Gusha is a gesture of welcome, or thanks.

Tejj is a wine made from honey.

The hand works like a claw, without the raptor's hurry, without welcome, and although for a time I could not swallow and did not want to be fed, neither did I refuse it.

I cannot say if my father is dead now, or if my father keeps living.

Another night, in a room in a hotel named for the empress on a hilltop in Addis Ababa, I dream again of middle Ohio, where I have never been. To reach the pond, I must walk through the field and through a copse of trees. Nights pass before the dream elaborates, before I reach the trees. In the shade of the first tree I reach is the body of a small horse, fully grown, no bigger than a schnauzer. The coat of the horse is a deep brackish gray, its mane cropped and silver, a red collar around its neck.

I used to dream only words—dark letters, evenly blocked, traversing at a steady speed across a blank screen.

Here is something true: In Addis Ababa, in the wake of some battle, the prisoners were made to march through the streets—these prisoners being mostly women—these women made to march through the streets, carrying the genitals of their husbands, of their fathers, and of their sons. I imagine these relics—enshrined, anointed, perhaps prayed to.

I tried to explain about *gusha*—my reluctance—that I did not wish to be fed. There was no such gesture in my country.

"In my country," I said, "the old feed themselves. The young go other places."

It occurred to me to wonder what language God would speak, if He spoke. He sitteth at the right hand of God. The son of God. Our Father. Jesus Christ was a black man rent from the womb of a woman. In Hebrew, Eve is "lady of the rib." In Sumerian, from which the Hebrew is translated, Eve is "lady of the rib" and "lady who makes live." In Hebrew, of course, the story is a simpler story.

In Addis Ababa, some twelve years after a girl is born, her clitoris, with a thin, curved knife, is cut from her.

I have heard it called a flower, the mouth of a woman.

Let me put my mouth on your flower.

Labia comes from the Latin word meaning "lips." *Clitoris* is from the Greek: "to shut." *Pudendum* comes also from the Latin, the gerundive of *pudēre,* "to cause shame."

In Mali, perhaps elsewhere—I only know what I know, what I have seen and what is written—the adulteress is given a cayenne-and-black-ant douche, and she is tethered to a stake in the village.

The goat bleated, the bigger boys astride its back. The small boy kept watching.

"In Mali," the man said. "But there is no such punishment here. Here is water, here is wine, bread. Please."

But I did not wish to be fed. The man's arm clenched and bloomed, pushed across the top of the table.

It happens, depending on the girl's father, some twelve years after the girl is born, that the entire labia majora is taken, cut away, washed with urine or spit, poulticed with the shit of ox—and who shoos flies from this, pinned butterfly-winged to some wall?

The men emerge from the shade, in the dream, made by the copse of trees I must pass before I reach the pond. They have killed, besides the small horse, a goat, and a heifer, which hangs by its neck from the branch of the tree.

Do you want to? the men say. They say it together, a chant. *Do you want to? Do you want to?*

The man stood up from his chair. A chair is a pile of burlap sacks wrapped with what string there is. The man was wearing a belt; worn blue trousers.

The goat stumbled on its tether, on the ball kicked back and forth by the boys through the goat's legs. It was not a ball quite, or at least it was not my idea of a ball, nor was the sound made the sound I knew of a bare foot and the skin of a ball meeting.

When I get there, the men are behind me; my father is inside. The doors are locked to the house.

Let me acknowledge these as human crimes, of largely indifferent significance—those of Addis Ababa, of Mali, of middle Ohio. Let me say I was no stranger then to the feel of a man at the back of my throat, to the clench and bloom of me.

I used to feed my father. I do not imagine it matters much if this is dream, recollection, hope, regret. He has grown quite thin, quite old. Without warning, as things happen in dreams and in life, my father's mouth is open, his eyes, but even as I feed him, he does not breathe.

I have not served him. The bed is narrow. It creaks.

They will come soon—those who come to bear the dead away. I am bleeding. My skirt is wide, drawn like a sheet across him.

It is a scene to me of such splendor, such ruin. I put my mouth to my father's mouth, my flower—and by God, by Christ, for the ways I cannot serve him, I bleed.

ABOUT THE AUTHOR

Noy Holland grew up in New Mexico and Kentucky. She has degrees from Middlebury College and the University of Florida, and is currently at work on a novel.

A NOTE ON THE TYPE

The text of this book was set in Garamond, a modern rendering of the type first cut by Claude Garamond (c. 1480–1561). Garamond was a pupil of Geoffroy Tory and is believed to have based his letters on the Venetian models, although he introduced a number of important differences, and it is to him we owe the letter which we know as "old style." He gave to his letters a certain elegance and a feeling of movement that won for their creator an immediate reputation and the patronage of Francis I of France.

Composed by PennSet, Inc., Bloomsburg, Pennsylvania
Printed and bound by the Haddon Craftsmen, Scranton, Pennsylvania

DESIGNED BY DOROTHY S. BAKER